Suite for Three Voices

Personal Narrative,
Short Story,
and Essay

Derek Furr

Fomite
Burlington, Vermont

ISBN-13: 978-1-937677-21-3
Library of Congress Number : 2012942155

Fomite
58 Peru Street
Burlington, VT 05401
www.fomitepress.com

Cover Art – Eric Olsen
Author Photo - Cecilia Maple

Contents

A Note to the Reader

Strictly speaking, the three voices of this suite are personal narrative, short fiction, and essay, with the fictional story coming second in each cluster except the Courante, where it is last. But *Suite for Three Voices* derives from my interest in the lyrical borderlands between essay and fiction, and each dance presents a variety of epiphany, an experience of second sight.

I gratefully acknowledge the following journals, where earlier forms of several pieces in this book first saw publication: *Gulf Coast, Potomac Review, Post Road Magazine, Literary Imagination, New Delta Review, Field Notes, Able Muse, The Literary Review,* and *Fourth Genre.*

Among the many friends and colleagues who played a role in this book, I want to name four: Donna Elberg, who gave me a column in *Field Notes,* read an earlier version of this book, and said "publish it"; Eric Miller, il miglior fabbro, the most generous of readers, whose many acts of kindness include a note that pulled me back from despair; Marc Estrin, who delighted in the idea of a mixed-genre book and helped me see what this one could be; and Caroline Ramaley, who started calling me "writer and teacher" on our tax returns years ago, a small gesture that seemed to make it official.

This book is dedicated to my family, who serve, perhaps more often than they like, as subjects as well as inspirations. It is dedicated in particular to the memory of my grandparents: John Smith, Linday Meggs, Harold Furr, and Faye Austin.

Prelude

Starting from Error

> "Make it a mistake"
> —Gertrude Stein, "Patriarchal Poetry"

"There is an e at the end of time," my student Samantha whispered to Tim, pointing out to her friend that he had spelled "time" as though he were writing his name. I peered over his shoulder at his smudged page:

> I whent to the Virginia beach with my mom
> and dad we stayed for the longest tim we at
> pizza and then. I when to lay down for a nap
> and then when I got up we whent back home
> and then I was taking a bath and when I got
> out of the tub we whent to the store and I got
> a cap gun and I played with it until the caps
> was out and then I throw it in the trash be-
> cause I did not need it to play with so I have
> not played with one since and I still don't.

"I know that," Tim snapped, but I asked him not to fix his misspelling. I copied the paragraph and have kept it all these years.

There is an e at the end of time.

If you are old enough you have experienced first hand the midnight passage from the Star Spangled Banner to the high-pitched electronic note that signals off-air until dawn. There's a wide-angle shot of Old Glory, as if you were standing under the flagpole and looking up. The flag flows—no snap, no flutter—in slow motion on a breeze made by trumpets. It's hypnotic, in part because you're exhausted, but the home of the brave ends abruptly and the color bars appear in shades of gray on your black and white TV. They're backed by a piercing "eeeeeeeee," and however much you dread the silence of midnight, it's preferable to that sound of no tomorrow.

"There's always tomorrow/ For your dreams to come true" crooned the claymation deer, big eyes like a Jersey cow and sweet voice to comfort all the misfit toys and Rudolph. In the right circumstances, I get a lump in my throat still. If you don't, you have perhaps put away childish things. But some of these you will retrieve, and others will return in spite of you. Tim never let go of the cap gun after he threw it away. How quickly it becomes present in tense and to hand: he played with it until the caps was out and then he throws it away, right now, again, as he writes. Memory in transcription slips into the present. When went becomes "goed" it's one thing, when it becomes "go" the child writes as (if) it happens. She is back in it.

It is six years since Samantha started me on this. I come back to it knowing it must end, whether or not I end it today as I write and listen. Upstairs and downstairs two kinds of music are playing. I tell you honestly, making no compromises for the sake of composition. Here at 5:48 PM upstairs is Ellen Taafe Zwilich's Chamber Symphony. Downstairs, my wife Caroline listens to Radio One Canada, Quebecois singer-songwriters. Between, my son Jacob slaps his plastic sword against the bedposts—he is sparring. Trucks pass slowly and steadily outside, muffled, a tidal flow. "As you near the beach you must roll down your windows to listen for the ocean. You will smell it first," my father says, "then you will hear it." We turn off the country music and listen quietly.

Now upstairs a Bach Partita for violin,

Nathan Milstein performing. There's an e at the end, she whispered, and it was a kind whisper, the voice of one who would spare her friend embarrassment and who has made such errors herself. She did not mention the e at the end of "ate." Neither she nor Tim noticed its absence. "we stayed for the longest tim we at…" Take away the e (ate − e = at) and be suspended in not quite place as well as not quite time. At where? At pizza and then. It's possible that being at pizza is like being at your best or at odds, that is to say, not so much a location as a state of being. He was "at pizza and then."

And then at 9:55 all of the students are lined up at the door. But as I notice this I think about the fact that even the door has moved, imperceptibly. Nothing here is still.

The e at the end of time must be the prelude to motion-lessness we can barely conceive of, a space with no when or went.

What if there were an "h" in "went," as there so often was in my students' writing? When is involved in went, time rolled up in the past tense, its graveclothes. Great-Grandma Meggs told us about the silver dollars they laid on little James Weaver's eyes when he died at three years old. On the mantle was the only picture of him, a tiny photograph the color of weak tea, and he was so small in it that you could make nothing of his expression, let alone his eyes. But there it was, along with the picture of her other son, Fordham, who died at 33, same as Jesus. Before they turned his body up from the flooded river on Mother's Day, he had looked like Errol Flynn. The muddy water of spring returns the skin to clay and spittle. "Those were pearls that were his eyes." Now I lay me down to sleep.

When to lay down (there is only one kind of lie in the South, having nothing to do with rest) given so little time? We had only a weekend at the beach, we had counted down to it all summer, and I knew it would begin to pass as soon as we unloaded the car at the hotel. I would hide my watch so that I could not see the second hand, but I always knew what time it was. I always know what time it is and will know when the note sounds to mark the final hour.

Which should not be played sostenuto on the violin, incidental music after Armageddon, but should be the full-throated happy oblivion of a chickadee, or the recording of a chickadee, the long-playing record version for warmth of tone.

Tim did not want to end time, he knew how to do it but forgot as language poured from him, his sentimental tale of endings, its momentum carrying him forward oblivious to tense and punctuation and spelling, and to the fact that at the end there is an e.

Allemande (Noli me tangere)

Within Reach

My grandmother's arthritic fingers would not straighten. Each knuckle was a marble, her palms were always cupped. To start a batch of biscuits, a daily routine, she built a hill of flour and excavated a pond in the middle for oil. Her hands resembled sand-bucket shovels, covered in a pale, powdery yellow. The powder seemed to have magical properties, because once the pond was filled, her fingers loosened ever so slightly, her hands began to scurry and burrow, cutting ditches and pinching small knolls until a ball formed perfectly between her palms. Now the transformation reversed, her fingers stiffened, and she dropped the ball onto a buttered baking tray to be rolled and sliced. Her biscuits came out rectangular and crusted, unique among the many biscuits by other hands in my family.

Imagine Grandma Delphia Flavelia after dinner with her autoharp. Her right hand sprouts talons, a claw more delicate than the hawk's and again surprisingly agile. The harp (actually a zither, says the ubiquitous and omniscient Wikipedia) shouldered, her bent left fingers spread just enough to secure a knuckle in the pit of each damper bar, the talons skim and pluck, skim and pluck. With its sharp metal strings and eight possible chords, her instrument established its musical horizons: not from the autoharp comes an intricate weave or Celtic twilight, but the speed, strum, and drive that became bluegrass and country music. Mother Maybelle Carter—her age-mate, same poverty, same faith, from the same hard-pine porch steps—was her sign of the possible.

My grandfather on the other side of the family, Papa John, had no right hand. My little brother and I imagined it cleanly severed, boxed, and buried in the Smith family section of the Pleasant Hill graveyard. Not as it was, ground in the silage machine like a Shielding's limb in Grendel's teeth, then nowhere we could trace it, maybe nowhere at all. Except that he felt it, his invisible useless right hand, its cold pain real as a rotting tooth. So he wrapped where it might have been in a sleeve-end. Warmth thawed his imaginary blood.

As for the left, retrained to a compensatory suppleness, it did all: whittling, writing, steering, hoeing, swinging the ax. In my family, he became a symbol of perseverance, though he had no time for such symbolism. His life was hard from beginning to grim ending, as too many lives are, and he would probably say, without irony, just play the hand you're dealt. We learn our limits, most of us, with some variation in timing and circumstance. How do we determine what's truly out of reach? Robert Browning's pitiable Andrea Del Sarto famously sighs, "Ah, but a man's reach should exceed his grasp/ Or what's a heaven for?" "You mean that that 'reach-versus-grasp' business is not a cliché but is Browning?!" a student of mine once asked, knowing quite well it could be both. The line tends to generate debate about the virtues of ambition and to betray how intolerant of failure most of us are. At best, the act of over-reaching shifts our limits, if slightly, just enough to keep us from throwing up our hands. So I tell myself, remembering my doggedly self-sufficient grandfather climbing a ladder to the barn roof and nailing tin back in place. If he teetered, he cussed the ladder.

Winston and Andrew, hosts of a radio show about Romantic piano music, close with Brahms, the A major Piano Intermezzo, op 118, no. 2. Andrew says that he has played the piece, then corrects himself, "I should say I've played at it." Winston echoes his "played at." None of us at the station is a concert pianist, he declares, but how many of us have returned time and again to a piece such as this? I nod at the radio. The three of us then listen to Stephen Kovacevich, joyfully, knowing that we'll never master it, this small wonder, at turns intensely introspective, declamatory, unsettled, and diaphanous. Even if our hands fully cooperate, the Intermezzo eludes them. We're on the porch steps with a toy piano, Kovacevich is inside at the grand. But that image of child's play, of playing at being a pianist, is not true to what we make of the Brahms each time we attempt it. We play at it, which is not to say we pretend to play it but that we go after it, coming close, approximating. We fall short, we are drawn again to the keyboard, some phrases do become ours. These we are playing, not just playing at. They enter not only our hearts but get fully under our hands, and we connect to a sound and its ideals. To cease playing at the piece is to settle along the border of pleasure, listening in.

Remember going to the beach when you were young. You kneel, your knees sink in the damp sand. You have your red shovel. When the next wave breaks, the crabs spill from it like beads from a necklace. You fix on one nearby who has begun his rapid descent toward the earth's core. Forgetting your shovel (it floats out to sea) you shove your fingers into the sand and give chase. A lake forms, constantly filling from the sides and top, seawater and sand, and it remains shallow, regardless of your speed. Another wave bears down, and the lake becomes a plain of quicksand. You swirl the muck from your fingers. As for the crab, a spirit, he has disappeared. You will dig for another.

In high school I became obsessed with the myth of Sisyphus. My enthusiasm for the myth came from the fact that it gave the lie to the faithful field-clearing of my Protestant upbringing. By way of example, here's the refrain of a Baptist hymn I often played as church pianist: (Sopranos) We'll work (Tenors) We'll work (Everyone) Till Jesus Comes / And we'll be gathered home. A good Baptist works hard because all hard work contributes to the building of the kingdom of God. I emphasize "hard" because difficulty, unpleasantness even, is fundamental. In a community of farmers, a kid often finds himself moving rocks, literally, though the task has many corollaries: digging holes, carting dead animals, shoveling manure. The rewards of such work come hereafter, if not in paradise, as it were, in the assurance that heavy lifting is good for the soul. The calluses on your hands were stigmata; men would ask to see your hands and nod with approval. Sisyphus, as I understood it at sixteen, aroused my suspicions of all this. Maybe there were always just more fields to clear, more piles of rocks to make. Maybe nothing ever grew in the open spaces, nothing that lasts, at any rate. In the words of a country music song popular in those days, "Work your fingers to the bone and what do you get? Boney fingers." People were doomed to roll boulders up a hill only to have them roll right back down like a feebly shot pinball. As a teenager will, I applied the phrase "it's a Sisyphean task" with undue frequency to a remarkable range of human activity. I read the works of Camus, not necessarily well but with intensity and earnestness. I bought my first black turtleneck. I sat in the dark.

Ironically, my newfound understanding of the futility of human efforts did not make me less driven, even if it caused me to question the inherent value of hard labor. On the contrary, for the tasks that actually mattered to me, I angrily set goals and dared my limitations to get in the way. Hearing Horowitz play Scriabin's D-Sharp Minor Etude, I declared to my best friend that I would learn to play it before graduation. Hard work and faith would surely put it within reach. If I felt the pulse of the etude along my own blood, couldn't my hands be trained to perform it? Over and over I grappled with those thundering, ascending sixteenth-note chords. Over and over I fumbled and fell, knocking rocks loose and scrambling to regain a hold before I hit the bottom. Perhaps it's needless to say I never got the etude in hand, and yet I don't recall exactly when I gave up. I admit that occasionally I try again, if only to be reminded of what it might be like to play the piece.

Disappointment rarely arrives empty-handed. But dissatisfaction is a hollow man, settled with his back to the horizon. As Browning recreates the tale, Andrea Del Sarto is widely admired and essentially dissatisfied. His belated realization is that superb handiwork has not brought him to the kingdom of heaven, so to speak, any more than indulgence has won him the heart of his unfaithful wife, Lucrezia. Browning casts Raphael and Michelangelo as artists to Andrea's master craftsman and has the lesser painter declare: "I am judged./ There burns a truer light of God in them,/ In their vexed, beating stuffed and stopped-up brain,/ Heart, or whate'er else, than goes on to prompt/ This low-pulsed forthright craftsman's hand of mine." The light comes second, dimmed, to Andrea. It comes to his hand, not his brain or heart or "whate'er else" might be the seat of passion. Andrea's list of adjectives is hardly flattering, betraying his envy of the confused, ecstatic state of inspired work that he cannot seem to enter. His reference to a "truer light" echoes the Gospel of John, the "true light" for the gospel-writer being Jesus. But in the end the faith of Browning's poem is not so much Christian as Romantic, setting art above craft but not separating it from work. Browning understands that inspiration comes unearned and, paradoxically, at significant cost. It is as likely to arise from work as to precede it—that is, from the meaningful work that sustains us, that makes the bread and the music, that sends a one-handed man up a ladder with his hammer. Whether in the name of Jesus or Sisyphus or nobody in particular, you'll work your fingers to the bone for what matters to you because it will otherwise never enter your grasp long enough to slip away.

Feed My Sheep

The first time I rode with Irene to the grocery store, which is something we've been doing together now for 15 years, I asked if I should lock her car doors when we parked.

"No ma'am, Gladys. Only thing worth stealing in this Plymouth is my Living Bible, and praise the Lord if somebody's tempted to take it!"

Now that's Irene, plain and simple. Doesn't lock her house either, because if Jesus had had a door, she says, he'd left it wide open, *especially* if there was trouble in the neighborhood.

So I shouldn't have been at all surprised when Irene stopped to pick up that hitchhiker.

We were on our way back from the new Ukrop's in Richmond. Irene likes to try grocery stores in the city whenever we can, even if it means a bit of a drive. "You see different people," she says, "and different food." To make it worth the extra mileage, we'd bought two weeks worth of groceries. We'd crammed plastic bags in every spare space of the yellow Duster, dry goods inside, frozen stuff in the trunk since it was cold out. Sunny, mind you, but bracing cold, the kind of day that can trick you into leaving the house in your shirt sleeves and coming back chilled to the bone. And I doubt it was much warmer in Irene's car than outside it. The heat in that car is like a tom cat, coming and going as it pleases, and so far on that trip, it hadn't turned up at all. I could see Irene's breath when she sang, which she does a lot in the car. There's this AM station that specializes in torchlight songs, and the Duster's radio has never tuned in another. Thing is, Irene has a magnificent voice, a cross between Peggy Lee and Dolly Parton. She was harmonizing with Sarah Vaughan on "April in Paris" when she spied the hitchhiker.

It was a girl, I'd say thirty-years-old at most, though we never found out for sure. She was wearing a muumuu covered with big red poppies. At a distance, she looked like a little girl in her mama's night gown. The muumuu was a tent on her, she was so sandpiper thin. She carried a duffel bag big enough that she could have crammed herself into it. Maybe she did, at nights.

Now I've been calling her a hitchhiker, but I don't recall her thumb being out. She was just standing there, her muumuu billowing and fluttering. The wind off the eighteen wheeler ahead of us might have launched her like a kite except for the weight of her duffel bag.

Even before I put a hand on that bag, I knew it weighed a ton. "Reckon she's got a La-Z-Boy in that bag?" I joked, though I could barely hear myself over the life insurance ad on the radio. "Maybe a reading lamp, too." But Irene didn't laugh. She was too focused. She turned the radio down. She was studying that girl intensely, giving her a story. That's what Irene does, always, when she's connecting with some lost soul. "Evicted from public housing," she whispered in that voice she gets when the Spirit has her under conviction, "after her drug-addicted boyfriend stole all the cash she'd made in tips and left her penniless when rent came due. She's on the street now, probably hitchhiking back to Mama. Probably hasn't eaten in days...look at those hollow cheeks."

When we were about 300 yards past her, Irene hit the emergency flashers, stopped, and put the car in reverse. We were going back, the engine whining and tires bouncing on and off the curb. Even though you could have seen it coming, even if you didn't know Irene, it startled me just the same. All these years and I still expect Irene to be more like me than herself. "I guess we're stopping?" I asked, knowing the answer full well.

Which Irene provided anyway, in her stern mother voice. She'd had plenty of practice with it: raising five boys, and all of them wound up to be straight-shooters. They're all happily married, even though their daddy was as worthless as the faux pearl earrings he gave to Irene right before he went out drinking on their fifth anniversary and came back in handcuffs for romping with the preacher's fifteen-year-old daughter.

"Why wouldn't I stop, Gladys?" Irene asked. She had the stern mother posture down, too. She loomed over you, and you became aware of how large she was, though most of the time you'd just say she was big-boned or matronly. "She's somebody in need. What would Jesus do?"

"How do we know she's not loopy, Irene? What if there's a gun in that bag?" I should have known better, but it's nearly impossible not to be cornered by Irene when you're being prudent.

Irene whooped like a revival preacher. "Well, praise God, Gladys, you've just given me all the more reason to stop! A soul so desperate as to shoot two penniless widows driving a beat up Duster needs the love of Christ more than both of us put together."

What could I say to that? Irene pulled up next to the poor creature and cut-off the engine.

Even on a sunny day, the highway from Richmond in winter is lifeless, everyone racing to put it behind himself and get somewhere less desolate. We must have been a sight: beat-up bright yellow Plymouth, lights flashing, picking up a stick figure in a muumuu. Seeing us on that gray highway must have been like a blip of samba when you're skimming the static on the car radio.

Irene reached across me and rolled the window down. "Sweetheart," she called, "can we help you get some place?"

The poor thing just stood there, right outside my window, and didn't move. She stared into the car, her eyes swimmy and vacant, as if what she was seeing hadn't quite registered on her brain yet. Her cheeks were sunken and her lips chewed and flaky. Her ears and fingers were blue, and when the wind cut through the car, I imagined that her poor naked body was like ice under that muumuu. The muumuu kept flying up to her bare knees and thighs, which were just as thin as broom straw, and she didn't even bother to cover up. Altogether, she was a pitiful sight. Except for her hair. It was corn silk, thick and tangled, reaching down to her waist. It made her head cock to one side, Crystal Gayle-like, and must have weighed as much as that mysterious duffel bag. I did feel for her—I'm not hard-hearted—but she spooked me.

Next thing you know, Irene, in her hot pink sweatsuit and blue crocheted cap, was out of the car and hovering over the poor wretch like a mother hen. She motioned for me to hop out, which I of course did.

"Now, sweetheart," Irene cooed, having switched from stern mother to coddling grandma. I don't mean to imply that it wasn't a genuine switch. Irene never fakes an emotion. "We're just going to help you into the car so we can drive you some place warm." Since Irene had her arms around the girl for support, I reached over to help carry the bag.

That's when the girl hissed.

Now Irene denies it, says anxious people like me are always hearing and seeing ghosts. She says the girl did no such thing, didn't even so much as sigh. But you'll just have to decide whether you're taking my word or hers. And I know what I saw and heard. That girl bared her canines like a cornered cat. You could feel her thin muscles clinch.

It was like when something dead suddenly rears up in a horror movie. My heart skipped a beat and I jumped back. Irene shot me her stern mother look again. I could read her mind: "How can you rescue the perishing if you're afraid of them?" Irene is unflappable. The girl could have breathed fire, and Irene would have calmly directed her to point her face away from the car.

"Why don't you put that heavy bag on the floor of the backseat?" she suggested, "then stretch out back there."

I started rearranging grocery bags, shoving several around my feet up front. I left the 24-roll pack of toilet paper for the girl to use as a pillow.

Some space cleared, the strange girl heaved her bag into the car. It moaned under the strain. Then she did exactly as Irene had encouraged. Slowly, as though she might break, she eased into the seat and pulled herself into a ball. Irene glanced at me again, so I shed my topcoat and spread it over the girl's feet. She was in flip-flops. Her toes were cracked and black. She smelled.

Irene crawled back in and took my hand stealthily. "Hospital," she mouthed, and pulled back out on the highway. She turned us around at the first service access road and headed us back north to Richmond.

With all the opening and closing of windows and doors, it was like a refrigerator in the car now, even with the third body. So Irene cranked the heat up to max, and for a change, it took a notion to blow hot air—wicked hot, in fact. That just worsened the stench that crept up from the back seat. I can still taste it in the back of my throat: urine, infected flesh, and the floral fragrance of shampooed hair. I gritted my teeth to choke back the nausea. Why hadn't she or whoever washed anything below her neck?

I was trying to dredge up fellow-feeling from somewhere in my heart, because of course I could see how desperate the poor thing was. But like I say she scared me and, I'm almost ashamed to admit, disgusted me. I've never been able to get next to a homeless person, or to any stray for that matter. Irene, on the other hand: how many cats do you think she has, and not a single one of them bought or without a defect? We had two grocery bags just for cat chow and litter.

I keep thinking that some of Irene's bound to rub off on me.

But right then, I was counting the minutes to Richmond, and praying for Irene to speed. Of course, Irene never speeds. It's partly the Duster—it starts to shimmy and shutter when you push it over 50 miles per hour. But it won't surprise you to learn that it's also in keeping with Irene's philosophy. "The Lord wants us where we are," she says. "And the faster you're going, the more focused you are on being some place else." At the moment, I was focused on it even though we were creeping along. But how could I complain? I haven't needed to ride a bus since I met Irene in the hospital 15 years ago. I can't drive, I've never owned a car. And the fact is that riding together every week is what's made me and Irene inseparable.

"Sweetheart, if you're starting to thaw a bit, I'll turn the heat down," Irene said. I guessed even she was finding the noxious mixture hard to bear. She switched off the heat.

With the grinding buzz of the fan gone, we noticed that the girl was mumbling. It was so soft you couldn't make out many words, but there was expression in it, like she was chanting. I thought about the demon-possessed in all the New Testament stories, and then about a witchcraft cult I'd seen on the talk shows. Irene glanced over at me. Her eyes sparkled like she'd just heard her child say its first word. Then she must have read my mind, because quick as that she turned stern again.

Irene was disappointed in me. I could sense it. When she's disappointed in you, it feels like something's leaking out of you at a great rate, something vital. Sometimes around Irene I get like a schoolgirl around her teacher. I can't stand being out of favor. So in spite of myself I spoke to the girl. "Ma'am, what's your name?" It kind of tumbled off my lips.

Imagine how shocked I was when she answered? Now, her answer didn't make any sense—it turns out to be what she said every time she spoke. Doubtless, it's what she had been chanting when she hexed us. "And when we were children," she answered, "staying at the arch-duke's, my cousin's, he took me out on a sled, and I was frightened. He said, 'Marie, Marie, hold on tight.' And down we went. In the mountains, there you feel free. I read much of the night, and go south in the winter."

Her voice was brittle and high, like a small child who's just woke up. Honestly, there was something almost pretty about the way she said this. But it was drowned out by the creepiness of the whole situation. She said that line over and over, as if she were practicing or trying to get her voice to work again. Then she stopped abruptly, and went stone silent.

For a moment, even Irene was speechless. The Duster rattles (Irene says it's spark knock), and that's all the sound there was, until Irene found a reply. "Marie, honey, I know what you mean about the mountains. The pace is slower there, like the Lord intended it to be. Do you still have family there?"

Marie didn't answer. I glanced over my shoulder. She was gnawing at her knuckle and whimpering softly. She had a hand on the duffel bag. When she saw me looking, she glared and hissed.

"Goodness, Marie, I didn't even think to offer you food!" Irene declared, as if she hadn't heard a thing. Believe me, those hisses weren't subtle. Spit sprayed from her lips. And her eyes were wild. "Gladys, poor Marie must be starving. Fish around my bags and get her a Moon Pie. I'll take one, too, while you're fishing. We just need to raise your blood sugar a bit, sweetheart. We'll get you a hot meal soon."

Irene's addicted to Moon Pies. She says it's her only vice—the sweet tooth—and at least Moon Pies are low fat. I found the box, unwrapped one, and laid it on the seat next to Marie, who was all curled up again, her face buried in blonde hair. I gave one to Irene, too, though it turned my stomach to imagine eating. The stench lingered.

Irene took a healthy bite and turned the radio back on. Julie Andrews was singing "My Favorite Things." It's one of Irene's specialties. The tiny speaker in the dashboard rattled, she had the volume so loud, and she sang as best she could through the Moon Pie crumbs.

It made me nervous to have my back to Marie. I kept imagining her heaving a butcher knife out of that duffel bag and plunging it into my head. But I was afraid to turn around, afraid of her demonic hiss. So I pulled down the passenger's visor and pretended to probe my eye for a stray lash. Marie was stroking the duffel bag and weeping quietly, as if it were her old collie and he'd just breathed his last. She was mumbling again, inaudibly. It was pitiful, and I felt for her, even if she did spook me.

Irene, meanwhile, was singing away. She believes that making a joyful noise is appropriate at any time. It reminded me of when Irene and I met. My husband had been dead about a month. He'd had cancer, and it had been a long, awful battle. I'd been right there with him every second, up to the end. Then it was over. Snap, like turning out a light. My daughter popped over to check on me one day on her lunch break and found me still in bed. I hadn't been up in days—I couldn't do it. Next thing you know I'm being admitted to the psychiatric ward at the hospital.

That's where I met Irene. Naturally, you know, she wasn't a patient. Irene's house is built on a rock if there ever was one. She was delivering hope bouquets—that's what she called them. She'd started a flower ministry at Word of Jesus Baptist Church. She'd get a list of new patients once a week—different floors each time, she'd have too many names otherwise. Then she and a small platoon of Women's Missionary Union ladies would take around simple arrangements with an evangelical note attached. Mine said, "Jesus wept, too." Irene brought it, marigolds and baby's breath. When I started sobbing, she sat right down and began singing. She did all of *Sound of Music*, stroking my head the whole time.

When Irene turned onto the exit ramp for the hospital, I glanced back in the mirror to see Marie's reaction. She didn't seem to register our slowing down. She was just staring blankly at the bag. The news came on, so Irene switched off the radio. She tried to get the heat going again, but it seemed that the heater had finally given up the ghost. It didn't so much as buzz or sputter. Pretty soon, you could see your breath, and you could hear Marie's low, steady mumbling. Over and over, she was chanting that sentence about the mountains and going south. "In the mountains, there you feel free. I read much of the night, and go south in the winter." It was like when old people talk to photographs, or to a mirage of somebody they loved. I'm not far passed retirement, but I've talked to ghosts of the folks who've gone before me. Maybe Marie was doing something like that.

We pulled up to the emergency room entrance. Irene twisted around to speak to Marie. "Sweetheart," she said, "I know all sorts of people here. They'll fix your sore feet, get you some warm food, set you right up. You just relax there and try that Moon Pie. I'll be right back with help."

I was leery of being alone in the car with Marie. What can I say? I got out with Irene. She shot me that stern mother look again, laced with disappointment. I stayed by the car, but I wouldn't get in.

A few minutes later, Irene came back with an attendant, a tall thin guy with a moustache. He was pushing a wheelchair. When he stooped way over to reach in for Marie, he looked like a giraffe going for water.

"Ah, Professor Eliot," he exclaimed. There was something not entirely kind about how he said this. "Miss Irene didn't say it was you! Headed south again, were you? You ought to wait till you're there before putting on a muumuu this year!"

He hoisted Marie out and into the wheelchair. I was shocked that she let him touch her. Of course, she kept a spindly hand attached with a rigor mortis grip to the handles of that duffel bag. The attendant heaved it out and across the arms of the chair.

"That's a good twenty pounds heavier than last time, Professor," he remarked. "You might want to conjure up a red wheelbarrow for your next trip." He chuckled in a self-satisfied sort of way. Irene intervened.

"Mr. George, if you'll kindly move over," she bumped him out of the way, indignantly. As I've said, Irene is no small lady. And she hates irony. "I'll wheel Marie inside."

She charged off with the poor creature, leaving me there with Mr. George. He looked perturbed and ashamed all at once. He was torn between telling Irene off and asking her forgiveness. I know this for a fact, because I've been in the same spot with Irene. You don't know whether to cuss or cry.

Unlike poor Mr. George, I felt a burden lift off of me as Marie disappeared into the hospital. But I was burning with curiosity about her, now that she was safely out of sight. Why had Mr. George called her "professor?" What was in the bag? I thought he might confide in me. After all, we had something in common—call it Irene-guilt.

But he ignored me and jogged off to help with the emergency. There was now a flurry of important-looking activity all around me, involving nurses and doctors, gurneys and bags of IV fluids. Fidgeting for something to make me look busy while I stood there waiting for Irene, I spied Marie's Moon Pie, untouched on the backseat. I reached in to throw it out, and that's when I noticed that Irene's Living Bible was missing.

When I told Irene, she shouted, "Praise the Lord!" That's just what she's like.

Who So List to Hunt, or
Poets and Deer in the Headlights

Struck in mid-leap by a northbound truck, the doe sailed, legs splayed, like a starfish tossed, or a paper helicopter spun, from the tips of a child's thumb and forefinger. She was awkward in flight, gangly like a blue heron, but her gracelessness was offset by her sudden lightness. She sailed several yards—in my memory, in slow motion—before sliding back into her weight in an ice-clotted ditch.

All of this I witnessed from one car's length behind the truck, such that as the doe spiraled downward, she seemed to peer through my windshield. Her eyes were opaque, already lifeless. At what point on her arc between first and final contact did her green soul—always without mass or weight—slip out?

Last time it had been different. The deer, whose eyes I stared into, whose life I grazed as I sped along the highway, had survived. On the road, close encounters with deer are too common, but there is something uncanny about the near repetition of the encounter I have in mind. I was driving my family back north through the Poconoes after we moved from Virginia to New York. It was late in the evening, and traffic was unusually heavy. In the lights of the truck ahead of me I saw a doe approach the shoulder of the road. I swerved before it leapt, landed parallel to our car, and bound back into the darkness. In the moment, the less-than-moment, that the doe stood by us, her slim face nearly brushed the driver's side window. She seemed to look in at me, her vast black eye vivid with sorrow and fear.

The eyes, the repetition, recall Freud's interpretation of E.T.A. Hoffman's "The Sandman," a source of his theory of the uncanny. Young Nathaniel is told the legend of a night creature who throws sand at unsleeping children so that their eyes leap out in pain, polliwogs squiggling on the bedroom floor. The poor insomniac is subsequently terrorized by the legend and its uncanny manifestations in his life: threats of blindness to him, visions of the blinding of others. Freud rationalizes the narrative's coincidences and tantalizing incongruities by deducing that the castration complex is its repressed subject. Reader, swerve away from the psychoanalytical explanation for now, and train your imagination on the eyes of Olympia, Nathaniel's beloved with the strangely illegible gaze. She turns out to be a beautifully made automaton. Her eyes are the handiwork of Coppola, one of several avatars of the Sandman. First we see Olympia's eyes enlarged by Nathaniel's telescope as he watches her from afar and the too-perfect eyes unwittingly seduce him. Next there are no eyes, only empty orbits (think of those mangled faces in Hitchcock's *The Birds*), their vile jelly cast at Nathaniel's feet when the poor boy learns that he's been duped. Finally, the wide innocent eyes, like those of a deer, stare up at Nathaniel from a crowded street. Olympia appears to be alive again, driving him to a final bout of madness. Nathaniel's experience of the uncanny is the experience of a gaze, now living, now lifeless, a mirror of his own mortality.

If you've had the misfortune of watching an animal die, you know something of this. Our dachshund Wagner (forgive the pun on "wag," we were young) was twelve when his cancer spread so widely that we were compelled to euthanize him—or "put him down," a euphemism with no ameliorating effects, as if death were an insult, a put down, or the baby brother you shouldn't have picked up. The veterinarian, who loved Wagner as we did, injected the Phenobarbital overdose, and Caroline and I talked to him. I watched Wagner's eyes. They were large, brown, and only calm when we were near, as now. And it's true what people say: you can see when life leaves, the instant when the creature cannot see to see. After he died, I couldn't keep looking in his eyes. They spoke things they shouldn't, of emptiness, of the Unheimlich.

The darkest realities are hidden on the surface. They manifest in our routines, seemingly out of nowhere but there all along, as we rushed forward or looked elsewhere. I run at dawn and frequently see deer feeding on the briars and wild strawberries by the roadside. Sensing my approach, they become alert, and in unison their heads turn with the quick, snapping motion of automatons, the window-dressing deer of Christmas in New York City. Without appearing to look directly at me, they see me, their seemingly averted gaze suggesting nonchalance, their eyes signaling the caution of all creatures that have evolved as prey. Once I spied a doe in the distance, and as I approached she stepped out of the brake and onto the road. It was foggy, and she appeared to be covered in a shawl with tassels, knotted and tangled, dangling below her belly. Something about her silent walk and gaze reminded me of the ballad verse, "Downe there comes a fallow doe/ As great with yong as she might goe./ She lift up his bloudy hed,/ And kist his wounds that were so red." But there was more of gothic than of mystic legend about my doe. As I drew close, the shawl and tassels proved to be a blanket of ticks, engorged to varying degrees, bulbous and wet as a hundred naked eyes in the satchel of the Sandman.

I must have shuddered; I certainly picked up the pace and kept my mind trained on the doe of the ballad. In the eyes of the mortally wounded knight, the fallow deer recognizes her false true lover, the oxymoronically named character common to traditional love ballads. Despite the suffering she has endured because of his neglect, she carries him to a lake to be buried, and she dies by his side. This is according to the earliest recorded version of the ballad "The Three Ravens." By the time that Walter Scott takes down another version two centuries later as "Twa Corbies," one raven has disappeared and the other two have become cynical. A man walking alone overhears "twa corbies" speculating about where they'll eat this evening. One suggests that a newly slain knight, abandoned by hound, hawk, and lady, will make a sweet meal: "Ye'll sit on his white hause-bane,/ And I'll pike out his bonny blue een./ Wi' ae lock o' his gowden hair,/ We'll theek our nest when it grows bare." Imagine the telescopic lens of the nature documentarian training on two scavengers, each with his own cup of blue jelly. There are no deer, symbolic or natural, in the corbies' vision. Their feasting on the knight's eyes is an uncanny, if oblique, comment on how he has looked on life with love, honor, faith.

That my close encounters with deer have been marked by the uncanny and the gothic runs counter to a figural tradition in which the deer is most often associated with romantic desire: its swift arrival, consuming pursuit, and as swift departure. The doe in particular is desire's object, his elegant, elusive paramour. "Who so list to hount," Wyatt famously declares, "I knowe where is an hynde." As figure, the hind arrives to Wyatt's sonnet, via Petrarch, already symbolic, swift but panting from centuries of coy evasions, a fact that is at least implicit in the speaker's enervated pathos. Gladly would he give up, he tells us, "Yet may I by no meanes my wearied mynde/ Drawe from the Diere: but as she fleeth afore,/ Faynting I folowe." Exhausted he passes the torch to us, her naïve aspirants, but not before warning us that our pursuit, too, will be in vain. She belongs to someone else—Caesar, in fact—so the law protects her. That aside, she is literally intangible, *Noli me tangere*, like the body of the resurrected Jesus, forbidden if tantalizing. And like the muse, she appears within reach while always remaining a step further away.

The object of Wyatt's hunt and the poet's pursuit is female, as she so often has been in the lyric conflation of erotic and artistic frustration. Art imitates the gender oppression and sexual violence of life, a pattern that later writers with a deer in their sights attempt to break. In real life, as opposed to art, a doe is generally not the deer hunter's target, a fact that makes Carol Frost's slaying of a doe in "To Kill a Deer" all the more startling. "Slaying," in fact, is too poetical a gerund. In the poem, Frost's speaker shoots and wounds a doe and, after taking on a doe's sensibility to aid in the subsequent pursuit, shoots her a second time to finish her off. We are witnesses as the hunter skins and guts the doe, breaks her legs, describes the smell of the meat. The hunter delights in the evisceration of this specifically female body, and her violent violation completed, s/he sighs, "Ah, I closed her eyes." I use the equivocal pronoun because Frost is carefully ambivalent in assigning a gender to the hunter, who is classically male but who, in this poem, is logically Frost, able to become "a woman with a doe's ears" and thereby sense where to find her quarry. Everyone who has made love or art is implicated in this hunt, the end of which is death, evisceration of a kind, decay. The pursuit is a process of trickery, a getting inside the head of another in order to possess it, and the love object made symbolic ceases to be unique. The metaphor of love as hunt, Frost suggests, stands to blind us to the violence of both, love and hunt. Like the poem's hunter, we know this, so we cannot abide the doe's dead eye. We close it and look away. But the poem ends not with vision but with sound, a terrifying "riot in the emptied head" of the deer that is too loud for the hunter or us to ignore.

It is no coincidence that my most violent encounter with a deer happened on a highway—that all three encounters, for that matter, were along roads. I venture to guess that you, too, have sped by the mangled carcass of a deer, its eye exposed to spray from the wet asphalt. Framed by your headlights, it's a contemporary version of the Dutch still life paintings so despised by the English Romantics, the exactly rendered brace of rabbits, art as a mirror, the soullessness of our quotidian brutality neither praised nor condemned. Roadkill is a fact of the driver's landscape, like a power line, which we don't notice unless it falls in our path. Never one to hold back his moral judgments, William Wordsworth imagined a divine natural justice whereby the land would waste around such scenes of cruelty toward "the meanest thing that feels." In the first part of his "Hart Leap Well," a knight breaks away from the hunt to give chase alone to a deer. Wordsworth suppresses the scene of the kill—in fact, he tells us he's doing so—because he wants us to focus on the knight's perversely exuberant response. The knight glorifies the "gallant Stag," and immediately renders its leaps spectacular and the chase legendary by engaging an artist to commemorate it with a fountain and monuments. The poem leaps forward in time to the 19th century for part two of the story. Wordsworth is on a walk and comes across the dried-up fountain, a decrepit monument in a barren coppice. A shepherd begins, and the poet finishes, the moral implied by this scene. Sympathy is natural, they assert; literally, nature responds in sympathy with the loss of a unique life and its experience of a particular place. For all his wonder at the deer's agility, the knight had not understood the creature's fear or pain and had been indifferent to his part in it. To insure that we take his point, Wordsworth warns us "Never to blend our pleasure or our pride/ With sorrow of the meanest thing that feels." Two centuries older, Wordsworth's moral is not otherwise far from Frost's. Her method—the unflinching cruelty of her speaker, the dark tone, the indirect reference to the figural tradition and its problems—may appeal more readily to us than Wordsworth's sentimentality and platitude, but both poems put us back on a path to the creature whose suffering should be our concern.

I say "on a path" because Frost and Wordsworth write within (however antithetically) the figural tradition of "The Three Ravens" and "Who so list to hunt," and their deer do more than graze, plainly, in plain view. It couldn't be otherwise for literary deer. Writing about my uncanny encounters, I cannot but make something of (or, like Frost, set you up to make something of) the doe. But that—the crafting and suggesting, the interpreting—is not in itself a liability on the actual creature or an indulgence on our part. Presented with the language of someone's experience, either you or I will set out to make sense of it, and an act of interpretation can be an act of sympathy. At its most successful, the literary figure causes us to slow down and look again, thoughtfully, at the creature as well as what she may represent. When we swerve on the highway to avoid the deer's carcass, we haven't been guilty of pursuing the hind, let alone striking it down. Rather, it's that we keep on driving, pursuing (instead) our interests, that implicates us in a coldness categorically similar to the knight's joy, the hunter's sadism, and the poet's wanton replication of a misogynistic trope. There are degrees of cruelty here, but our self-serving forward motion paves across many an animal's bones.

In none of my roadside encounters did I stop. I kept moving, a pace to maintain or an appointment to keep. So now I force myself to look again in the lifeless eye, then the startled eye, then the wary eye of three does I've passed, connecting them by more than coincidence. I depend on emotion recollected in tranquility, as Wordsworth put it, which also suggests that my account is indirect. For me, perhaps for all writers, it travels through the analogous written experience of others. I imagine that this began in the moment of my initial response, almost simultaneous with it. For how soon after I saw the SUV launch that doe did William Stafford's "Traveling Through the Dark" enter my mind? Have I ever seen a deer without hearing Herbert Howells' setting of the 42nd Psalm? My experience of the doe's blank gaze may have been uncanny without Freud, but an experience is only as arresting as the language that attends and shapes it. We return because we were brought up short. There was not time or space to accommodate the words we felt.

The repugnance of an uncanny experience rebounds paradoxically into sympathy, which always creeps along the edges of our fears. We shudder and look away from the sufferer, but our mind's eye turns back to her, places us alongside or even inside her. Wordsworth considered this to be natural; we should hope that it's at least human. In the poem "A Secret Gratitude," James Wright suggests as much. He recalls walking with friends on a winter's afternoon and spotting five deer. We assume that the setting is near Austerlitz, New York, because the poem begins with an allusion to Edna St. Vincent Millay, who lived there for most of her adult life. Wright's text has a dream-like quality that juxtaposes the encounter with the deer, Wright's dark reflections on the suicide and suicidal tendency of his friends, and the image of Millay tidying her house before she died. A longing to feel sympathy—actually, to feel at all—organizes the dream, and while there is no direct reference to it, Millay's "A Buck in the Snow" is the presiding spirit. Much of Wright's poem is steeped in self-loathing and misanthropy. He describes himself and his friends as "chemical accidents of horror," alcoholic and suicidal. Men, he declares, are all essentially killers: "We can kill anything/ We can kill our own bodies." At first sight, the deer merely remind him of this, perhaps in part because of Millay's lyric, in which a buck, wounded by a hunter, is left to die in the snow. But that lyric also leads him to imagine a scene of human sympathy. Millay's poem ends with a doe waiting expectantly and alone in the snowfall, with "Life, looking out attentive" from her eyes. In a similar vein, Wright imagines Millay hovering over the body of her husband, whose death is described as a falling "down like the plumes of new snow." The faint echo of Millay's poem that Wright hears in his snowy encounter with the deer rebounds to his poem's opening lines and re-frames them: "She cleaned house, then lay down long/ On the long stair." Millay prepares for death and then lies down with it, but her doing so, Wright implies, was a show of love, an act of sympathy with Boissevain.

Wright's admiration of Millay is hardly unqualified; he describes her as a Daphne "who could turn into a laurel tree/ Whenever she felt like it," surely a back-handed compliment from a suffering poet. And whether suicidal or not, Millay died of a severe concussion after her drunken fall down the stairs of her ostentatious home. But Wright recovers from this gothic spectacle—and momentarily from the maudlin melancholy of his own experience—by traveling through the gaze of the frightened deer and into the sad heart of a misunderstood, if laurelled, poet. His vision of Millay's pathetic end, its frightening solitude in her unheimlich home, clarifies into a sign of the human capacity to grieve and create.

I have waited until now to admit that I come from a family of deer hunters. When hunting deer became legal again in the area of North Carolina where I grew up, my father and uncles were jubilant. Tree stands and blinds were constructed, corn and salt licks strategically positioned. I received a Winchester rifle for Christmas, the lever-action kind, Matt Dillon style.

I never shot a deer, never even aimed at one. Neither did my father. This was not for lack of opportunity. Our failure as deerslayers sheds light on our embarrassing enthusiasm when the laws changed. "I couldn't shoot something so beautiful," my father says, "except with a camera." Hunting simply provided a rationale for the luxury of rising before dawn not for work but to go into the woods and wait quietly. A sighting would be different from driving by deer on the road to the factory or fields. We would have no other destination, no need to brake or swerve. There would be no chase, nothing to pursue besides the chance encounter, the sight of a deer in the lifting fog. We would just watch.

But under those circumstances, I never saw one, perhaps because I never went to the woods with so little apparent purpose. I tend to lie awake afraid of the Sandman and rise early to get around the next bend. I regret what falls, most of us do, but I keep going. Most of us do. When we've outrun our fear, or it has caught up with us, when we've arrived at our destination only to find that it's further than we thought, what does the soul, finally, pant after? In the end, I might wish I had put aside my pursuits, stopped the car, and lingered with the creature in its final moment.

Gavotte I (The grave thick with voices)

Tabula Rasa

In the month before Thanksgiving, Papa Harold had told my father all his stories over and over. "He'll tell you one," Daddy explained to me, irritated, "then not five minutes later, tell it again." My father and I were feeding his handful of Black Angus steers, and without ever looking directly at me, he was trying to prepare me for the changes in my grandfather. I was back home in Pleasant Hill, North Carolina, for Thanksgiving, the first time since the birth of my second son over a year before. When I'd last seen Papa Harold, he had been characteristically ebullient, telling tales of babies he had known as he amazed my son Samuel, then a toddler, by popping his false teeth in and out. But he was now suffering from a rapidly degenerative form of senile dementia, which in just a few weeks had erased his short-term memory.

Now, my father continued, Papa Harold couldn't recall that he'd just eaten or checked the mail, or that he had just recounted that old chestnut, the story of his dancing paint horse. "At least a half dozen times I've heard it," Daddy sighed, dumping the feed over the noses of the bellowing steers. However, Papa Harold's recall of the distant past was pellucid; it was as if, unclouded by the quotidian—those minute-by-minute trifles that necessarily occupy the mind—the memories of his childhood regained their original candlepower.

Alas for my father, Papa Harold's stories only served to exacerbate the tedium of having to be his father's string around the finger. The dementia had come on suddenly and had completely altered my family's life. Best we could reconstruct it, Papa Harold had become disoriented in the woodworking shop where he'd spent most every day since retiring at age 79 from the textile mill. Not able to locate the saw he held in his hand, he'd become increasingly agitated until, furious, he'd grabbed an ax and cut into the electrical service line. The flash had singed his hair and pitched him like an oily rag into a scrap pile across the room.

Almost daily since that episode dropped my family into the maze of the medical establishment, daddy had chauffeured his father forty miles from home to (depending on the day of the week) the family doctor, the neurologist, the cardiologist, the urologist, the pharmacy, the grocery store, or Bojangle's, the dining option of choice on every excursion. With my father at the wheel, an eighty mile round trip in a pickup truck on the windy narrow roads around home gave my grandfather a captive audience and an intimate space for his story telling. "It's like listening to a broken record," Daddy complained.

I asked Daddy what stories Papa Harold told. Fetching a walnut from his coat pocket, he cracked it in his fist and shrugged. "You know, the ones he's always told. That damned paint horse and the rest."

There were many. I asked, "Which of the others?"

Daddy sighed. He cracked another walnut, and picked the nuggets out with his pocketknife. He studied the walnut awkwardly as he spoke, blushing "Derek, I got to admit, I don't recall. I tuned him out."

Ignoring Papa Harold, even at the best of times, would have been challenging. He was a big man, in stature, voice, and personality. Tall, thick-limbed, husky, with tremendous feet and hairy hands, Papa Harold stooped when he stood or walked, as if the sheer mass of his features was a burden to bear, and filled the cab of daddy's small pickup on those long rides. He was loquacious and loud, jovial and emotional. He played with my brother and me when we were small, got down on his knees and pushed fire trucks and screeched for their sirens. Director of the church choir, he crooned in a fine, untrained and untrammeled tenor voice. He spoke to strangers. He wept openly, both in joy and sorrow. And he told stories that were unique in their naïve humor—indeed, in their complete lack of irony. When he poked fun, he himself was the target. Even before the dementia, there were stories he told again and again, such as his "eating" stories at Thanksgiving. He loved to tell them, and we loved to hear them.

"In them days, now, your grandpa could do some eatin'!" As if to punctuate this line, which always led off and concluded his "eating" stories, Papa Harold would serve himself a third, generous slice of sweet potato pie, hoist it with his thick sticky fingers, and consume it in three bites. Papa Harold was a big eater, and breakfast, dinner, and supper all required biscuits and meat. By noon of each day, a new pie was expected. My red-haired grandmother, whose florid character demands its own essay, never took off her apron. At Thanksgiving, I've watched Papa Harold ingest a turkey breast, several slices of ham and fried chicken livers, a bowl of creamed potatoes with red-eye gravy, stuffing, squash, yams, crowder peas, and a half dozen biscuits. All this after Grandma Faye's rural variety of hors d'oeuvres: sweet pickles, hoop cheese, and walnuts. With his feast, he'd drink a quart jar full of buttermilk before setting forth on the pies. Fully focused on placating his voracious appetite, he spoke only directives during most of dinner—"reach me a biscuit," or "spoon me some taters, please." But after the second slice of pie, he'd rear back in the chair, stretching his belly for one final push, and exclaim, "In them days, now, your grandpa could do some eatin'!"

"Them days" were when he was a child, a "whipper-snapper" as he'd say, growing up poor like everyone else in rural Pleasant Hill in the 1920s. His family raised or hunted the food they ate, made the clothes they wore. They scraped together a living by farming a few acres of cotton and raising pigs, cattle, chickens, turkeys, rabbits, hounds—any animal that might be sold or traded. His father was handy with wood and tools, so occasionally the family would rate a salted ham hock or a bag of onions and potatoes in exchange for a coffin or ax handles. Papa Harold's memories of the Depression seemed to be fairly typical, except that he almost never mentioned going hungry. For him, the purpose of remembering and telling was to be filled again, not to be left hollow or cold.

His only story of hunger was really about satisfying it, indeed satiating it, and annually concluded Thanksgiving dinner. He was about eight years old, he'd recall, beanpole thin and always eating. Our great-great-granddaddy Burgess, he'd say, had been working him and his sisters to death in the cotton fields, till finally Papa Harold just had to sneak away, he was so famished and parched, even though he knew it'd be the strap when he was caught. He crept back over the hill to the old plank house where his Granny Burgess was baking pies for the church revival that started the next day. Anxious about his granny's reaction to his leaving the field, he just lay at first under the window on the porch, shaded by a giant elm and taunted by the aroma of cinnamon and dried apples. But he couldn't stand it for long. Gaunt, dirty, and pathetic, he stumbled through the door and startled Granny, who was overwhelmed with pity just by the sight of him. "Child, is that old man trying to work you plumb to death?" she cried. Fussing about like a hen, she ferried Papa Harold to the table without even demanding that he wash his hands. One pie finished, she took it from the cooling rack and placed it before my grandfather, along with a knife, fork, and plate. She cut him a steaming wedge, then trotted to the icebox, pulled out a gallon of buttermilk and set it with a pint jar in front of him. "Now, you just help yourself, child,"

Granny's voice dripped with sympathy. "I got three more in the making for tomorrow."

"Now, lord, I remember every bite!" Papa Harold would sing, rubbing his stuffed paunch. "That was the best eatin' I ever had. Et that first slice, washed her down with a pint of buttermilk, then I et another. Soon enough I'd et the whole pie and drunk the whole gallon, and I was full as a tick. Granny Burgess looked surprised to see that pie pan licked clean and all her buttermilk drunk, but she didn't say a word against it. Took up for me with your Great-Great-Granddaddy Burgess, too…. Dried apple pies and buttermilk, that's good eatin'. Mmmm, lord, in them days, your grandpa could do some eatin'."

My father said that, in the final week before Thanksgiving, Papa Harold told tales non-stop—through his food, in the bathroom, as he fell asleep. He talked incessantly and in a circle, a large loop that described an increasingly predictable path through his favorite personal narratives. At times, he seemed unaware that he was talking, as though he were an oracle, the stories retelling themselves through him. I have a sentimental, perhaps foolish, theory about this. At any given moment, we are the sum of the stories we remember; life after death comes to those whose stories endure. His mind melting away like snow, Papa Harold's soul made a bid for self-preservation: tell all the stories now, over and over, to someone who won't let them pass away.

The story loop always began and ended—or, more

accurately, began and began again—with his paint horse. When Papa Harold was thirteen, his father gave him a paint horse. He traded their best mule and a day's work repairing a barn roof to Old Man Austin, who owned the colt and who, ironically, would one day be Papa Harold's father-in-law. The gesture was as grand as the gift was extravagant, for on a subsistence farm like theirs, a riding horse was superfluous, even wasteful. Papa Harold never told the story without tearing up at the mention of his father. "Weren't no use for that horse," he would say, then clear his throat to keep down the tears, "except to please me." Papa Harold raised the paint himself, hand-fed it hay on cold days, brushed it and picked the cockleburs from its tail. On Sundays, when no God-fearing Baptist would dare lift a finger unless the ox were in the ditch, he would roam for miles across the country, down the cliffs and ravines, through the acres of scaleybark, hickory, and loblolly that even in the 1930s had not yet been touched. Inspired by the B westerns that he watched for a nickel in Oakboro on rainy Saturdays, he trained the paint to do trick riding. It was the tricks that became the focal point of his story.

"Now, even when he was a young whippersnapper, your grandpa was a load on that paint's back," he'd laugh. 'But Scout, she was a good girl and aimed to please, and I reckon we got right good at the tricks." Papa Harold's favorite was an imitation of the Lone Ranger, in which Scout would dance about on her hind legs while the proud rider waved his straw hat. He perfected the trick with his sisters as audience. He asked for their critique: Was he graceful enough? Did he seem confident? Strong? He needed input, for he had a plan. Autumn would bring the big corn shucking at the Austin's place, where he would have an audience of dozens. Papa Harold intended to ride the paint to that event and, after all the work was done, show off his horsemanship to Old Man Austin's daughters.

"A corn-shucking was like a big party," he'd explain, "except you was working without really realizing it." Men and boys would shuck corn and chop fodder for feed all day. Women and girls would quilt and prepare the huge supper. Then, at around four in the afternoon, there'd be music—the Austins were famous pickers—dancing, food, and, for those in the know, Old Man Austin's corn liquor. All this continued past sundown by firelight. "Now it was about the time they got them fires lit that your Grandpa decided to show off. Somewhere in the Bible, Jesus says, 'Pride goeth before a fall,' and your grandpa learned it the hard way."

Old Man Austin had twelve children and, at this point in his romancing career, Papa Harold had his cap set for any of the daughters who were older than twelve. All the girls were redheads, thin as rails, and spunky. They went barefoot, dipped snuff, and stuck together like a chain of paper dolls. That night, they wore green gingham dresses cut from the same bolt and stitched at night while Old Man Austin read from the Bible or almanac. When the whole community had gathered along the porch and fence line by the bonfire light to hear the daughters sing as their mother played the Autoharp, Papa Harold decided to make his debut.

"Lord, it must have been a sight. Them girls all dolled up, your grandma was one of them, just setting off on the first verse of 'The Great Speckled Bird,' when here your grandpa comes, trotting up on Scout, rearing her up and getting her dancing to the music. Everybody was gasping or clapping, depending on how they felt about it, and them girls just kept right on singing, as if it was all planned and I was part of the show. Everything's jim-dandy—then your grandpa takes a crazy notion to stand up in the saddle. Well, you know how that turned out!"

In telling his story, grandpa would pantomime his fall with any available, nonbreakable object—a fork, his comb, his cap, your cap.

"Landed smack on top of your grandma and your aunt Ruby. You heard of falling *for* a girl. Your grandpa fell *on* her first! And your grandma's been making him pay for it ever since!" He'd chuckle, pat grandma on the shoulder, then head back to the kitchen for a snack.

It's common as you reach middle age to joke about forgetfulness. But being forgetful is different from being unable to remember. After multiple visits to a host of specialists, Papa Harold and all of us learned little more than we knew after our first visit—his confusion and forgetfulness were the initial manifestations of a degenerative condition. His short-term memory would go first, then he would forget names, faces, places, stories. In the end, he would lose the desire and ability to speak, move, and eat. All this loss, and yet one of the cruel ironies of the condition is that the autonomic nervous system is unaffected. Lungs breathe, heart beats, blood circulates. Food digests, when the sufferer is prompted to eat. Life in its most rudimentary form continues, though the self has vanished.

Leaning on a cane, refusing Grandma's arm, Papa Harold cautiously made his way from Daddy's truck along the short gravel walkway to my brother's back porch. His body was wintry and sparse. In the cold wind, his overalls billowed on his frame. My father had bought new, smaller clothes for him, but Papa Harold had protested against wearing them. They weren't his, he'd argued, choosing instead his uniform from the textile-knitting mill where he'd worked all his life, even after retirement, as a machinist. His cap, a discard from the mill, read, "I ♥ Dog My!" He had a rack full of such caps, and a closet full of slightly flawed overalls, now several sizes too large for him.

It was strange to see him outside the two acres of his home place. To take the pressure off my grandmother, who would have spent days preparing for a house full of family, my brother had offered to host Thanksgiving, and my mother had made the food. So for the first time in their long married lives, Papa Harold and Grandma Faye had left home for Thanksgiving. No doubt it was disorienting, but the look of bewilderment that my grandfather wore as he tottered up the path, fixated on the placement of his cane, had a deeper source. The very act of walking, it seemed, had become a mental puzzle. He was right in front of me before he noticed me standing under the porch light, with our one-year-old son, Jacob, clamped to my hip. At first he just stared blankly. Then something about his eyes—a glint of recognition, perhaps—suggested addled cogitation. He quivered. Tears began to well up, and his head shook. Unable to find words, spluttering sadly, he grabbed my hand and squeezed, brushed Jacob's belly, and choked back a sob.

Then, abruptly, all signs of emotion vanished. His face was blank again, and he staggered on up the porch steps. Jacob cooed and squealed and pulled at my ear. For several minutes, I stood listening to him play with his voice, attempting words, and I imagined the webs of meaning, intricate and gossamer, forming in his mind.

Thanksgiving dinner was conversationless. Papa Harold had to be reminded to eat, which he did mechanically, until my father determined he'd had enough and led him to the television set.

"He still likes watching it," my grandmother announced and turned on "Wheel of Fortune" before scurrying off to help with the dishes.

Uncertain how to behave or what to say, I sat and watched him. Could he decipher the mystery words or were his eyes merely mirrors, reflecting the jumble of letters? He didn't react to the buzzers and bells of the show, or to the blasts of guitars from the commercials. I wanted to turn it off and try talking to him, but what would I say? Besides, would such a gesture be taken the wrong way, as a commentary on how he was being cared for? Quietly, I talked myself into remaining inert. Lost children often stand still, hoping to be found.

Thus was I relieved when Jacob waddled over, chanting consonants. He climbed the sofa and broke up the blaring monotony of "Wheel of Fortune" by stealing Papa Harold's cap. It seemed to wake him. Papa Harold took the cap back, put it on, then bowed to let Jacob steal it again. A game ensued. Papa Harold was being playful, *deliberately* playful, I thought, and in his sunken eyes was that glint I had noted earlier. I looked at my father, who was studying the game in amazement. I took heart. At a pause in the antics, I placed a hand on Papa Harold's shoulder and said, "Tell us the one about the paint horse!" It was as if I hadn't spoken. He panted, and his eyes glazed over when Jacob returned for another round.

There were no stories that evening.

Alice's Big Break

Part the First

Alice

Wants to sing R. Strauss at the Met. Currently sings Cole Porter, Richard Rodgers, Gershwin and so forth for respectable pay in city night clubs. Worries that there's little to distinguish her from other talented vocalists, that she has no gift or that her gift is common. Has begun to settle, reluctantly, for what works.[1]

Jack

Drinks, plays, and composes. Is sure of his genius, that it is misunderstood, though in fact he is really no genius at all and rates little sympathy in this story.[2] Would be a recognized composer, he swears over scotch, if he could just get recognized. Wants to compose a nuanced, lyrical, yet postmodern piece that fully inhabits and extends Alice's voice. Hasn't yet. Does he love Alice? It's unclear. Her voice how-

---

[1] For three musical moments in Alice's development as insecure artist, see Appendix.

[2] Here we betray our intolerance for the pretentious and for alcoholism in artists.

ever transfixes him, and he is sure that his gift is unique.

They are

The two of them on Tuesdays and Thursdays at La Bohème, a French bistro in Harlem, managed by a clever Haitian entrepreneur, Toussaint, who loves opera and wants Alice to get a break. Toussaint specializes in all forms of mimicry, from obvious sham to winking kitsch. Bohème is patronized by the professionally rich who (1) have been fooled by Bohème's apparent authenticity, (2) are indifferent to authenticity but like Cole Porter and blanquette de veau, or (3) enjoy the mimicry as mimicry and are themselves masquerading. The sweet old man who will become important to our story falls into category one. Alice and Jack's schedule: 8-9, 9:30-10:30, 10:45-11:30, encore.

Alice in daylight

Barista at coffee shop. Always late. Awakens next to Jack, rolls off mattress into panties, tights, long black skirt, sweater, scarf. Runs. Fortunately for her, espresso is free to the workers.[3]

What changed?

Alice's prospects after Elijah's offer. An elderly patron

---

[3] "Fortunately" draws our attention not only to the fact that Alice will get caffeine despite her late rising, but also to the fact that espresso is overpriced in the current vogue of the coffee shop, preventing the truly impoverished artist from enjoying that storied site of artistic exchange, the café. A real, undiscovered artist cannot be found there, unless she's mixing lattes, as in Alice's case.

of Bohème whose wife is terminally ill, Elijah comes to the coffee shop on a Wednesday. Silk blue blazer, extra wide checked yellow tie, Bassett hound eyes. He is holding a thick, manila envelope.

Elijah: "Toussaint said I could find you here. Your voice. Transfixing."

Alice thanks Elijah awkwardly.

Elijah: "You can sing Strauss?"

Alice speaks for several minutes, digressive but unabashedly enthusiastic. She imagines the Metropolitan Opera House.

Elijah: "Night of November first, you and Jack perform *Vier Letzte Lieder* at my house. There are conditions. They are written on the contract in the envelope. You will also find there an advance on your payment."

What conditions?

Perform all four. Come and go precisely as directed. Tell no one what you see.

What money?

$100,000. 10K in advance, in cash.

What does Alice do?

Leaves work immediately to carry the news to Jack.

Alice and Jack consider

Positives include

Alice performs Strauss.

Alice quits coffee shop.

Jack able to fund his artist's life.

Little old man seems sweet and needy.

<u>Negatives include</u>
Mysterious "Tell no one what you saw."

Did they accept?

Yes, and agreed not to speculate on what they would see.

Two weeks later, Elijah's place

Brownstone. Butler. Twelve elderly people, mostly couples. Lots of talc, costume jewelry, silk. Alice positioned by baby grand Steinway.

Meet Elijah's dying wife

Mrs. Elijah (Muriel) wheeled in during opening bars of "Frühling." She sits awkwardly in the wheelchair, as if her thin arms and legs had broken loose with pain and gathered themselves pell-mell back to her distended abdomen.

Is it not true that Alice and Muriel were transported by the opening bars of "Frühling"?

That is correct. It's Muriel's favorite. As for Alice: had she not first heard the Strauss sung by Jessye Norman at the Proms in the Royal Albert Hall over a decade before? And had she not in those moments discovered her forbidden love for Rosaline?

Rosaline is

sculptor, dredlocks, fragrance of yeast and musk, intense not unlike Jack but with fellow-feeling and humility. Whom fate had placed beside Alice at the rail of the gallery and who likewise was hearing *Vier Letzte Lieder* for the first time. So began three years of struggle in art and love, lovely, artful struggle, subsidized by Rosaline's trust fund and Alice's under-the-table-cash-only singing gigs.

Oh death where is thy sting?

In Rosaline, who floats Ophelia-like among the mist and reeds of Alice's Strauss-induced vision. Rosaline, unannotated suicide in the Thames, foggy November evening. For Alice, there had been nothing to do but leave London.

Oh death where else is thy sting?

In Muriel.

Is that what Alice actually saw at Elijah's apartment, the sting of death in Muriel?

A gathering of friends, sated with bread and wine, gazing in loving admiration at Muriel, who is crumpled in pain yet seeming already to be breaking free of her body with the help of Alice's voice and the sting—specifically, 200mg of morphine injected by Muriel's physician. Wie sind wir wandermüde, Is dies etwa der Tod?

Jack and Alice told no one?

They were hurried out by the butler, who handed them an envelope and—drawing a finger dramatically across his neck—reminded them to forget what they'd witnessed.

Part the Second
The Hauntings

Jack and Alice were surprisingly successful at forgetting Muriel, though for Alice the side effect of such carefully practiced forgetting was remembering Rosaline. Nothing, she learned, is ever fully remembered, while much is completely forgotten.

Take Rosaline, for example. Alice could not recall the sound of her voice. That's right, Alice, a vocalist, for whom life was less an operatic narrative than a cantata of voices strung loosely around an idea. Rosaline's smell (clay and cigarettes), Rosaline's taste (sour soil), the textures of Rosaline's skin (newborn around her insignificant breasts and belly, becoming gradually sandier as you moved across her bony shoulders and down her arms to her horned, callused hands)—all of this Alice remembered as clearly as she could expect three years after Rosaline's death. But when Rosaline's ghost began to appear to Alice—at rehearsals, on the bus, in the bathroom mirror late in the evening—the countenance spoke of remorse and hopelessness and earnest need; the lips moved, but there was no sound.

{Enter the ghost of Rosaline. Ghost sits in Alice's line of vision.}

Alice: Rosaline! Rosaline! Never shake your dreadful locks at me!

Conductor: Ms. Fenwick? Are you quite well, dear? Should we break?

Alice: No, sir, she just won't talk, so how can I know what she needs?

Conductor: Who, Ms. Fenwick? Orchestra—15 minute break, and my undying gratitude to someone who brings me back a double latte.

Actually it happened more like this:

Final rehearsal of *Messiah*, St. Luke's Church, small but very respectable baroque choir and orchestra. On rehearsal evenings, St. Luke's had become an unofficial shelter for the homeless in the area. Cold and cavernous, the faux-gothic building was nonetheless cozier than the street in December, so that Alice had a small audience for "He Shall Feed His Flock." They gathered in the shadows of the narthex, a handful being bold enough to venture onto pews. Absorbed in the music, Alice was only vaguely aware of them, until Rosaline appeared. She sat alone in the pew nearest the shrine to the Blessed Virgin, light from the bank of votive candles spilling across her bare shoulders and breasts. Alice gasped. The orchestra tottered and stopped.

"Ms. Fenwick, is there a problem?"

There was dread in the conductor's voice, as if he were witnessing the catastrophe that he'd imagined with a pessimist's black-and-white accuracy.

Alice shook her head and cleared her throat. Rosaline was still there, her eyes like frosted window panes. She was talking to Alice without sound. Alice asked if the aria could be run through again. The orchestra obliged. Alice sang. In the twinkling of an eye, Rosaline disappeared.

Why is Rosaline haunting Alice?

One might surmise that Alice's repressed guilt has begun to surface. Despite years of therapy, she continues to imagine herself partly responsible for Rosaline's suicide: should have noticed Rosaline's unhappiness, shouldn't have been so emotionally demanding, should have given more of herself, etc. Furthermore, having only recently been an unwitting accomplice in the assisted-suicide of Muriel, and having worked to erase that memory, Alice's redoubled guilt manifests in the voiceless ghost of her dead lover.

Alternately, if we suspend our disbelief and assume Rosaline to be a real ghost, we might speculate that she has only recently learned to haunt.[4] That Rosaline has begun to haunt Alice so close on the heels of Muriel's demise is purely coincidental.

Did she haunt often?

With the fervor of a child who has learned to whistle.

---

[4] According to leading authorities on the subject, haunting requires the spirit to channel the electromagnetic fields of the live body of the haunted. Becoming visible is a highly skilled mode of haunting, second only to speaking directly to the haunted. To learn any form of haunting, Rosaline's spirit would have to observe other, more skilled spirits and imitate them, though she would not have the benefit of questioning them, for ghosts cannot communicate with each other. Consequently, the learning curve is steeper.

Initially, her visitations were always public—at restaurants, concerts, dentist's office—and were startling each time. Then there was a lull of four days[5], followed by…

Rosaline in the mirror

Alice awoke and stared at the red numbers of the clock radio until they came into focus. 2:45. She felt in the bed for Jack, though she expected that, as usual, he was draped across the piano keys or collapsed in the La-Z-Boy, deep in a double-malt coma.[6] She stepped out into the darkness, and as if in proof of how frequently of late she'd trod this path in the pitch dark at 2:45, rounded the foot of the bed at full sail, skillfully shot the strait between Jack's two permanent piles of dirty laundry, and reached the window without foundering.

Now she would draw back the curtains and crack a

---

[5] This is a common procedure with ghosts. Withdraw in order to create tension and speculation, then return abruptly in a new, unexpected setting. Banquo's ghost knew this well and used it to striking effect.

[6] **Why is he drunk?**
Can't compose.
Since when has Jack become unable to compose?
Since the move to the middle class. Had he not composed his "Jazz Improvisations on the Poetry of Catullus"—a piece so magnificently complex that the world was not yet ready for it— in his moldy basement grotto in Harlem? Destitution and its attendant detritus are fertile soil. Life emerges from the fen. An artist who tidies or, worse, concerns himself with furniture kills the germ of creativity.

window. Night air and street noise would lull her to sleep. Light from the eternal day of the city below would keep her company.

Tonight however there were flashing lights, and the noise included sirens close by. Alice peered out. Two police cars and an ambulance crowded the intersection at the end of her block. She stared for a few minutes, thoughtlessly, before her eyes began to cloud over. She turned back to bed, passing the full-length mirror as she turned.

Hers was not the only reflection there. Rosaline stood by the bed. Her skin was gray, her gaze exhausted. She was wet, a small pool forming beneath the dripping trench coat that she'd worn to her suicide. She didn't try to speak this time. She seemed to be waiting for Alice to begin.

Fearfully, Alice turned toward the bed. No Rosaline. She was still in the mirror, however, lit up by the flashing red from the sirens below.

"Rosaline, why are you doing this to me?"

The siren's wail had faded. There was no sound in the apartment. Rosaline's coat dripped noiselessly.

"Rosaline, please. I tried for so long to understand why you did it. I loved you. I told you every day. But you took yourself from me." Alice turned again toward the bed, but Rosaline was not there, only in the mirror.

"Rosaline, speak to me or leave. You said nothing when you left me alone in the rain three years ago. I've tried enough to imagine what you might have said. It's your turn to talk."

There was a knock at the door.

Part the Third
Another Bohemian Death

Who's there?

Detective Roy Martinique, 6'4", dark-skinned, earnest eyes, enormous hands. Wearing a trench coat.

Officer Glenda Mason, 5'3", fair, serious eyes, capable hands. Wearing a black slicker.

Do they come in?

Yes, after Alice (called 'Ma'am' by Martinique) invited them in a quivering voice.

What's the news?

Jack lies in the storm drain one block away. C.O.D. not yet clear. Strong odor of alcohol.[7] Found by Officer Mason on her beat. Traced to Alice by Martinique, an occasional patron of La Bohème.

How does Alice react?

There is uncanny silence. She returns to her spot before the mirror and stares. Officer Mason, in her role as comforter, follows. As she passes in front of the mirror, she starts, clutching her pistol.

---

[7] One is reminded here of Poe, whose death by alcohol and gutter is emblematic. We had originally written "Jack lies Poe-like." However, the appropriateness of the allusion is questionable, Poe having been a true artist at times as well as a parody of one at all times, Jack being mainly parody.

"I thought this was a mirror?"

It is.

"It can't be. Who's the strange dripping lady?"

That would be Rosaline's ghost.

"Who is Rosaline?"

Read part the second.

"Detective Martinique, take a look at this."

How does Detective Martinique react?

Unflappable, Martinique stares, nods knowingly, and offers his explanation. "Clearly this mirror is a literary device. We will need to examine it, Jack's body and Alice's psychiatric state. We will then need to review all of the results in light of Officer Mason's reading of part the second."

Will Officer Mason pick up on Muriel's role?

Among Glenda's recommendations to the police academy is a letter from Professor Margaret McKnight of Border College. McKnight was Glenda's advisor in her undergraduate major in English and writes of Glenda's "analytical thinking," "close attention to detail," and "perseverance." We are confident that the subtexts of part the second will be apparent to Officer Mason.

Back to Alice.

Is she trembling?

Yes.

Does Alice now scream?

Predictably, many times, rents her night gown, tears her hair. A paramedic is summoned.

What was that crash?

Alice tackling the mirror, Martinique tackling Alice.

Part the Fourth
Philanthropy

Meanwhile, Elijah finds himself wandering through mists lit by a thousand fireflies. He is disoriented, yet blissful. His heart leaps up, literally, lifting him above the mists and onto a mountain where thousands of people lounge. As if by an ineluctable force he is pulled to one among that crowd. His one. His Muriel.

They greet each other with tears and shouts of joy, echoed by a chorus of such magnitude and sublime harmony that Elijah knows it must be angelic. He wonders aloud how he has come here. Muriel explains that he collapsed before the main course at La Bohème. Massive heart attack. Alas for their daughter, who had been his dining companion and who had now seen both parents die within a year. But with their combined forces here in eternity, she and Elijah might be able to persuade an angel to visit and comfort their daughter. They should also consider doing the same for that poor soprano.

Elijah did not respond. He was captivated by the sheer number of souls popping up from the mists below, dozens every second. Had there been a natural disaster or perhaps a nuclear event down below? Muriel cleared her throat sternly, for even in heaven one does not appreciate being ignored. Elijah apologized and asked, "What soprano?"

Muriel now reminded him of Alice's wondrous performance on the night that Muriel crossed over. She told of Alice's subsequent sorrows; of Rosaline's spirit, condemned to wander in the mists for at least 9,997 more years or until someone here pled convincingly for her, poor thing; of the pianist's death ironically just this same night and how unlikely it was that his soul would ever make it out of the earth's atmosphere. Muriel sighed, for an angelic visitation was the very least that poor Alice deserved.

Now Elijah wore the intense, pensive expression familiar to members of the board of his company. He asked if the heavenly hosts might be able to arrange a Metropolitan debut for Alice. *Elektra* was on next season's bill. Perhaps the scheduled soprano could meet with an accident. Nothing permanently debilitating, of course.

Muriel smiled at her husband, for he had always sought to help others by using his considerable influence. It could be, she speculated, that if the two of them made the case to Father Abraham himself, such a debut could be arranged.

"Excellent. So where do we find Father Abraham?"

"Why, love, we're resting even now in his bosom!"

Only then did Elijah realize that the mountainside was in fact a giant belly.

Part the Last

Elektra

"Ms. Thompson's deft handling of the demanding lead role deserves the highest praise. Her acting was no less powerful than her singing, which is high commendation indeed, for her singing is unmatched, in our estimation, among recent divas of the technically and emotionally challenging modern repertoire." Review of *Elektra*, Times, Nov. 19

"We'll want her in the choir. That voice is a rare gift." Angelic choirmaster, letter to Father Abraham.

"It's what she always wanted, and would have never gotten with me around." Rosaline, from conversation in heaven with Muriel, who pled for her.

"I could have written great things for that voice." Jack, in purgatory.

Elektra's eyes widen, as though she has seen the ghost of her brother. Then she falls to her knees, for it is Orestes in the flesh standing before her.

Orest! Orest! Orest!

Es rührt sich niemand! O Lass deine Augen

mich sein, Traumbild, mir geschenkles

Traumbild, schöner als alle Traum!

(No one is stirring! Oh let my eyes gaze at you, a vision in a dream, a vision granted to me, fairer than any dream!)

"Yes, I've had difficult times. But when I'm on stage, I become Elektra. I always could have, I think, even if I hadn't been through hell." Alice Thompson, interview for *Vanity Fair*, Nov. 26

Appendix
Moments Musicaux from Alice's childhood and adolescence

{Cue Brian Wilson "In My Room"}

Alice kneels by her bedroom window with her Barbie. Snow has fallen on the plains, snow is still falling. Only the slightest change of hue—a small degree of grayness—distinguishes ground from sky. Alice and her Barbie search for the clothesline, Tom cat's gravestone, the bluebird box on the fence post, but all have been buried. Alice presses her forehead into the cold pane and begins singing with Brian Wilson. Her Barbie dances lightly on the sill and into the air.

{Cue "Pass It On" from *New Praises Songbook*}

Juniors and seniors own the back of the bus. Alice is a sophomore but she is allowed because she's a girl, she sings, and she lets David Fowler cop a feel. David is in the FFA crew, the boys in royal blue corduroy who smoke and play hearts in the last row. He rests his arm on the back of the seat where Alice is carefully, safely positioned between Jennifer Scanlon and Lilith McIlheney. She is glad that her breasts are difficult for David to reach, through no evident fault of hers, for Jenni and Lil had insisted she sit between them, soprano flanked by two altos. They sound great —"that's how it is with God's love/ Once you've experienced it…"—and security, song, and spirituality lift Alice for a moment out of the nagging concern that David will be angry.

{Cue George Crumb's setting of "De donde vienes, amor, mi nino?" by Federico Garcia Lorca}

"Alice, your singing is technically superior to any student I've had. But you're not suffering, and for this song you must suffer. You have not embodied the mad mother who sings it. You must live her hysteria at the loss of her child. Your voice is not crazed, it is an imitation of crazed. Put your self in a dark place with no distractions and say these lyrics to yourself, sing them until you become part of them. You are young, you have had no such experience and God forbid you ever do, but you must become the song. An artist can do this thing."

So we find Alice in a darkened listening room in the basement of the college music department. Her ears throb under the vinyl green headphones. We are outside the soundproof glass, yet we can hear, distinctly, Crumb's threnody on the lyrics of Garcia Lorca. Alice holds a small pen light over a photograph in a library book: a young Japanese girl, her face contorted in shock, her clothes burned away by the heat of the atom bomb, runs toward the camera. Sorrow builds in Alice's throat.

Elizabeth Barrett Browning
on the Resurrection Ship

The purpose of poetry is to remind us
how difficult it is to remain just one person,
for our house is open, there are no keys in the doors,
and invisible guests come in and out at will.
--Czeslaw Milosz

In sixth grade I had a Battlestar Galactica lunchbox, like the ones now going for $60 on eBay: aluminum yellow and black, inspired by the original, short-lived series that attempted to capitalize on the Star Wars craze. In those days Cylons were plump as well as shiny. The leading men had the colorful plastic shimmer of amphetamine capsules and the locks of late 70's porn stars. When I learned, belatedly, of the 2004 series, I cajoled Caroline into renting it. We became addicts, ravenous consumers of videopium, Jonesing while we waited for the next disc from Netflix on our one-at-a-time, budget plan. We loved the silly, slyly allusive names like Starbuck and Adama. We were suckers for the nostalgia for being offline—series moral: Only Disconnect. We fully indulged in the Cylon guessing game: you, too, or your best beloved, could be a bot in human vestments. And for me, a lapsed fundamentalist, there was the fantasy of a Resurrection Ship, its wired embryonic vats like Kenneth Branagh's bizarre *Frankenstein* remix. For what had the Cylons done but instrumentalize the ancient human hope of another round, that when the end comes it won't be an end? Technology or prayer, technology and prayer, will reanimate the traces.

So data must be stored in anticipation of the resurrection, our relics deposited in ever-more-sophisticated reliquaries. As a graduate student in the early 90's, when "desktop" was just beginning to be synonymous with "computer," I had a summer job boxing library books that no one had read in several decades—19th century anatomy textbooks, treatises on phrenology and galvanism, hundreds of monographs in the Q's and R's of the Library of Congress classification system. Many of these had been temporarily entombed in the attic of a dormitory, where the humid Julys and Augusts of the American South were speeding their deterioration. After being boxed, they would be shipped to a new storage facility, a technologically advanced version of the crate that Caroline and I packed and labeled "Photos Too Bad to Display, but Too Important to Throw Away" when we downsized to an even cheaper apartment that same penurious summer. My colleague in the attic, a fellow student freckled like me with flakes of decayed paper, called the facility a climate-controlled sarcophagus. I thought of it as a sperm bank of obsolete knowledge and obscure belles-lettres. For the librarian who'd hired us could no doubt imagine a future day on which a scholar would need just that inquiry into animating dead tissue to infuse his moribund dissertation with life. I mean no irony by this example. Was not my own dissertation conceived at a microfilm reader? All this has happened before and will happen again, as the Cylons knew, having taken a cue from Ecclesiastes, "the thing that hath been, it is that which shall be; and that which is done is that which shall be done: and there is nothing new under the sun." In a cardboard box with a barcode is the relic of several years in a life, the remains of a question, a pursuit, an answer, and finally the satisfaction that comes from completion, the final stage before being forgotten.

Forgotten but not gone. We could be crushed by the density of invisible guests who crowd any room, whispering all they knew and considered important. On a typical day that summer, I make my way from the attic to the reference room and my gestating dissertation, at this stage a clutter of notecards on Victorian women poets and Lord Byron. "His grave is thick with voices," wrote the 18-year-old Elizabeth Barrett, daring to be smitten by the naughty English bard, now dead but no less threatening in his virile atheism, mirror image of her other dearly beloved, her Calvinist father Edward. Crumpled into her chair at Hope End, where she will be confined for years by her mysterious illnesses, she eats her small spoonful of laudanum and hears those voices, the mourners, the critics, the lovers and haters, the host of suffering characters Byron created, avatars of himself. I scroll to her page in *The Globe and Traveller* newspaper, the gears of the microfilm reader marking time with a satisfying thump unmatched by either today's scrolling word processor or its papyrus precursors. Who else read this—I mean this very page in its first incarnation, the newsprint? What canny humanist packrat saved it from a newspaper's usual fates—fire-starter, fish wrapper—so it could now be resurrected in the overbearing brightness of the microfilm reader? I imagine the light of the machine is the young Elizabeth's light, searing, not to go unnoticed.

Twenty years later, after purchasing the *Battlestar Galactica* (2004) box set from Amazon for my father, aged 68, I recall Elizabeth Barrett's ghosts. Why? Because as I scroll down my list of recently viewed items, I click on an anthology of Victorian poetry I had considered adopting for one of my courses, and from the sidebar I learn that customers who bought this item also liked Elizabeth Barrett's collected poems. Reader, this is a process familiar to you: from the thumbnail image of the Penguin Barrett, a combination of my memory, chance, and hyperlinks lands me among Elizabeth's letters to her sister, Henrietta. A seer of ghosts and participant in séances, a believer, unpersuaded by her husband's skepticism, Elizabeth composes a messy, earnest apologia for spiritualism in these letters. "For myself I should like much to be able to tell you all, everything I know," she declares at the height of her faith in the invisible world, "but I can't yet at least. As might be supposed, all connections (social connections) perish—for instance French and Italian spirits will *tutoyer* and call by the Christian name everyone in the flesh: but for the rest, minute individualities, ways of speech and manners, are as much untouched by what we call death, as by putting off a cloak." She is not being facetious: these European familiars (does she think of the pun?) have lost the finer points of decorum, but crossing over has changed nothing else. She has been "touched by the invisible," she writes, and she means it literally. At a séance, she has been crowned with a garland by hands "as white as snow, and very beautiful." She hears the counter-arguments of her husband and friends. She even seeks them out and listens closely to the evidence of skullduggery, hidden accomplices, and sleight of hand. After all, the greatest of the mediums, David Dunglass Home, is a consumptive from the land of gold diggers, America. How can he be trusted in dimly lit, heavily curtained rooms? All this she knows, and some she accepts. But there is more in heaven and earth, she maintains, a "nearness and consciousness beyond what any of you have any notion—there is less separation—I stop myself. A few years more, and these things will be received as a matter of common opinion..." She could not resist claiming that the kingdom was at hand, because she writes not of the return of the dead but of their constant presence, one that responds to those willing to acknowledge it. So many had gone before her—the mother, the father; her brother Samuel malarial in Jamaica, land of the familial sins; her brother Edward the dearly beloved, drowned on the Devonshire coast, where they had moved for Elizabeth's health. Soon Henrietta, too, will pre-decease her. They cannot have gone far, she declares. She will not be numb to their presence, she feels their hands on her hem, in her palm, against her cheek.

If I whisper their names today, November 1ˢ, might they be present in the room? Here insert the final verse of "For All the Saints," the lower registers of the pipe organ causing you to stumble if not tremble, the sopranos' descant otherworldly and arresting unless your heart has already stopped, too hard to move. Allow me to set the scene as it really is today, All Saint's Day, at Clinton Avenue Methodist. Having only a Baldwin piano and a ragtag choir of six from the streets, we rely on imagination and earnestness and the fact that among the forty who have shown up for church, all have known loss, most are or have been addicted or poor, which redoubles the pain of bereavement, and all can speak the name of a ghost. We come to the part of the service where people say those names. Listen to them, name upon name, each representing an entire life: the breath, the first and last steps, the sleeping and waking, the now exact number of seconds during which the details of a self were made, those "minute individualities." There's not enough time to recall them all, and even still the room teems with invisible guests, the sibilance of their soft greetings. If I said "Elizabeth Barrett Browning"—said it and meant it—would she come? The grave is thick with voices.

This has happened before, will happen again. I am clutching my Battlestar Galactica lunchbox. Homeroom is preternaturally silent. Ms. C, whose voice always quivers, announces that a classmate, Flora Mae, has passed away. Hodgkin's disease. There will be a bus to the funeral. It's sixth grade, we're all new here, temporary residents, as everyone is throughout middle school, that nebulous, transitional space. We hardly know each other. But Flora Mae's corn rows, her surprisingly husky voice, her jump shot, then the large bandage behind her earlobe, its contrast with her sunken cheek—they are suddenly as present to me as the cold aluminum pressed against my t-shirt. "You should sign up for the bus." It must be my conscience that says this. I have been taught about still, small voices. But at the funeral the casket will be open. I don't want to see her dead body. "Still, you should go." I hear it again. My superego is as Victorian as the Brownings, as resolute as a Cylon. The right thing is to go. When the notepad comes my way, I clutch the lunchbox tighter and don't sign up.

It is difficult to remain one person, but the one who didn't sign up has not disappeared. Neither, Elizabeth would insist, have any of those he encountered. Even in my mid-40's, I avert my eyes from coffins, hearses, funeral homes. I turn away from pictures of people who died young or tragically. In the attic next to my Battlestar lunchbox is a stack of middle and high school annuals. I am struck by how many of my schoolmates never made it to grade twelve, a few of them like Flora Mae for reasons that cause me to tremble and turn the page. In the climate extremes of our old basement apartment, the pages began to yellow and crumble, not unlike many of the photos that were too bad to display but too important to discard. Everyone is vaporizing, the faces are barely distinguishable. Elizabeth, are you sure they're still here? Who is that behind me in the class photo, hovering over my shoulder?

Aging at the dawn of photography, dead before Edison recorded her husband's faltering recitation of "How They Brought the Good News From Ghent to Aix," *Then the gates shut behind us, the light sank to rest… I'm terribly sorry but I can't remember my own verses*, Elizabeth imagined something more constant than memory or mechanical representation. I say, "imagined," because I have less faith than she. Even as a child, I fretted over the details of the resurrection of the dead preached at us on Sunday morning, Sunday evening, Wednesday night. If the dead rise upon Christ's return, what about decay? What about the shark-eaten sailors in the South Pacific, or astronauts exploded in the atmosphere? "And though worms destroy this body," boldly sings the soprano, "yet in my flesh shall I see God." I put aside my skepticism for a moment and come on board the Resurrection Ship, spirit medium for the digital age. The Cylons' machine does an end-run around doubt by invoking our current faith in genetic manipulation and the indestructibility of electronic data. So the soul of dying Sharon (humanoid Cylon #8, AKA Boomer and Athena), along with her memory, zips across the vacuum, through some tubes, and voila fully intact into new flesh, cloned presumably from her DNA. The alternative to this, or something like it, being oblivion, every generation finds a new way to imagine an afterlife. The dead are reborn not in the guts of the living but in their busy hands and strong-willed imaginations.

Scroll down more slowly, please. That thump, thump,

thump is the machine's heartbeat. In every brightly lit page of film—each a reduction of a photograph of a typescript of a manuscript—there are many voices, many hands. I stared into the light until I saw Elizabeth Barrett. Now I am there, too, on this Resurrection Ship, with my Battlestar lunchbox and Flora Mae, Number Eight and another face I may yet identify. Invisible guests come in and out at will—my will and, it would seem, their own. Yes, there is a fading away, but for the rest, minute individualities, ways of speech and manners, the singular turn of phrase, the vision, the spark. It is difficult to remain just one person. It may not be impossible for a person to remain.

Sarabande ('Mid the torture of the scene)

Yellow Pajamas

The last time I saw Papa John, about three weeks before cancer finished the remnants of his visceral organs, he was in pajamas—yellow pajamas, cotton, with marigold trim. My grandmother Linday was there, too, in the shadows behind him. It was a Saturday, my grandparents' fifty-first wedding anniversary. Withered and gnarled, my grandfather was hunched over in his recliner, his hands drawn into the cuffs of his sleeves, his knees pulled tight against his chest. Jaundice had stained his sunken cheeks. The blue of his terrified eyes floated, absurd, in the color of daffodils.

I was flummoxed by this encounter for many reasons, but all of them were concentrated in the fact of my grandfather—the brooding and sometimes severe patriarch of my mother's side of the family—in pajamas. I had spent much of my life under Papa John's roof, and had only seen him in two stages of dress: fully covered in Pointer brand overalls—the kind worn by railroad engineers in children's books—and stark naked. Coming in from the barn at the end of the day, he would strip down on the back porch, shower, and blaze through the living room, a vapor trail of Ivory soap and red clay following him. He was shameless in his strong, hairy body, which filled the recliner as he ate his bowl of mashed potatoes and watched *Gunsmoke*. That's where he'd often sleep, naked and full, until he woke the next morning and, pulling on his overalls, headed back to work.

When I was little, I had once asked Papa John why he never wore pajamas. He spat a stream of tobacco juice into the bucket by his chair, reached over and turned up Matt Dillon before he chuckled, "They get all twisted and bind me up." My grandfather was not a man to be shackled. He made his own way among the hills and swamps of our tiny, rural community. He pursued his interests, acted on his whims. He moonshined and fished with dynamite. He raised barns, dug wells, cleared acres of pine for a sawmill he built of spare parts and sheer determination. He could grow any plant in creation, and his acres of vegetable gardens—irrigated by a complex system of pipe, pumps and ponds that he'd devised—overfed the twenty of us in his clan. When he was angry, he destroyed things; when happy, he laughed himself into paroxysms of coughing. We regarded him with the fearful respect that sustains gods and kings.

So finding him in yellow pajamas, his eyes swollen with hapless tears, I wanted to turn away. It was as if I had walked in on something that I shouldn't see, something forbidden. I thought of Lear, in his torn white gown, his countenance frozen in a look of disbelief, blubbering piteously over his daughter's lifeless body. For a moment, Lear doesn't know we're there, and should we be? What can you say or do when you see someone so reduced?

Illness and injury often humble us, shaming us into

acknowledging our limitations. But Papa John had always scoffed at pain. He rarely went to the doctor and never took medicine. Most aches or ailments could be ignored altogether, he suggested, and even the most grievous conditions could be endured with true grit and, perhaps, a few shots of Wild Turkey. About a decade before I was born, Papa John's right arm was cut off by a silage cutter. "Chewed" would be the more appropriate verb, for as he tried to dislodge a knot of silage from the machine's throat, it sucked him in and ground to a halt at his elbow, not sated but choked again. In the trauma ward for days thereafter, my grandfather refused to be treated for pain. "You get dependent on those drugs," he declared, and no amount of suffering was going to steal his rugged independence. At least not until the end stages of cancer.

On that Saturday, I nodded to him and awkwardly slipped away to a corner of the room that was partially blocked from view by the wood stove. The rest of our family began to crowd in, all of them from just down the road and bearing dishes of various descriptions for the potluck. Because I had traveled several hundred miles to return home for the first time in months, my presence provided some distraction—welcomed, I imagined, as a momentary ballast to suffering and disillusionment.

For a while my aunts and mother chattered about my weight, or lack of it, and the circles under my eyes, about how I needed to eat more and stop staying up so late reading books and worrying. Caroline assumed the yoke of the good partner—mediating between spouse and family —

and steered the conversation away from my health, offering up anecdotes about our drive down with our neurotic dachshund howling in the back seat. Most of us chuckled. Among the women, only my grandmother remained silent, vigilantly on call behind Papa John, the only man who hadn't at least smiled or blushed at Caroline's monologue. Then with sighs and winks, all the women save Grandma retreated to the kitchen, and the men of my family were left to their own, limited conversational devices.

My father and three uncles, each leaning back in a wooden chair dragged from the kitchen, stared awkwardly at their empty hands. My brother pretended to study a seed catalog that he had plucked from the otherwise empty magazine rack. Finally, Uncle Wes inquired, "How's the weather up north?" My home at that time in Charlottesville, Virginia, was "the north" to my family, a peculiar land of harsh winters and impractical ambitions.

"We've had our share of it!" I declared, and my uncle nodded. The silence resumed, denser now for having resisted our paltry attempt to fill it. The tocks of the clock on the mantle plopped into it like stones in a lake. Everyone stared holes in his hands. Tucked safely behind the stove, I stole glimpses at my grandfather.

It was now that Papa John had always saved us in the past. He'd get a story started. First he'd toss out an apparently artless observation about farming or hunting or mechanics. "The dry rot's going to eat up half the tomato crop this year." "Deer's been using the hollow. Got the bark rubbed clean off that big cedar." "Head gasket on the

GMC needs replacing." Invariably, someone would rise to the bait, giving Papa John a moment to light a cigarette—Camels, filterless, their fine Turkish blend holding the mysteries of the Orient. He would inhale long and deep while, for example, my father described the buck he'd jumped when walking the fence line, and then he'd exhale two billowing streams of aromatic smoke from his nostrils. A haze would gather in the room, soporific, even a bit intoxicating, and Papa John would deftly pick up a thread from my father's disquisition and spin it into a yarn from his past.

Today, however, it was as if that past had been razed and burned by the cancer. Those shanty towns of fops and shrews who populated Papa John's irreverent version of our family history were smoke and ash. He had no stories to tell—intense suffering had pinned him to the present. He stared at the window shades, a flinch and an attenuated cough his only vital signs. Grandma lingered behind him, an apparition, like his broken spirit.

Simply sitting in the presence of pain takes discipline. I squirmed. The temptation to narrative in such circumstances is understandable. Was it up to me, I wondered, to get a story going? Narrative organizes, interprets, distracts. For those very reasons, however, it had no place here. Job's companions should have just kept their mouths shut. I settled into the darkness.

But then a cake was brought in. The piping, the butter cream roses, the cursive wishes for a "Happy Fifty First," all were yellow. And on a tiny porcelain plate in the center were two gold wedding bands. Caroline ran ahead of the cake like a scout. She crouched by my knees and squeezed my hand, as she does when the plane hits turbulence on its descent.

And that's as much of the day as I can remember. My memory's stage goes dark just as Caroline clutches my hand, and the cake, like the Ark of the Covenant in its uncanny symbolic heft, is borne in. In truth, some time in the years that intervened between that day and my recollection of it, I even lost the rings. The cake I still saw, but the rings—which promise to focus the sad plot of that anniversary gathering, to complicate it and drive it irrevocably forward—were gone. Instead, it was the ruins of my grandfather, tricked up so absurdly in the colors of spring, that filled the day's space in my memory. The wedding bands reappeared in the rubble only after Caroline, reading an earlier version of this essay, pointed them out to me.

My grandparents had been too poor to afford the extravagance of rings when they'd eloped on Papa John's furlough from the army. They'd been too practical to consider buying them later. Love, they believed, inheres in the sacrifices you make for the well-being of your family. Doing without carries more weight than gold.

My mother produced the anniversary gathering and insisted upon wedding bands. She was determined to lay claim to joy despite the omnipresence of sorrow, and she wanted in particular to do something to bolster Grandma. For under the influence of intractable misery during his dying days, Papa John had been relentlessly cruel to

Grandma. Pain had whipped his demons into a fury. A man of his era, he unleashed them on his wife, who fussed at his sheets and pillows and freshened his watery Coca-Cola in a futile attempt to comfort him. Grandma had endured, but her daughter, understandably, agonized. "Mama must not feel unloved," my mother thought, "not now." Plans were made. A cake was baked and decorated. Rings were bought.

I don't recall the look on Grandma's face, or whether she and Papa John cut the cake. Did they feed it to each other? And the wedding bands—were they worn? Was one on Papa John's hand at his wake a few weeks later? There's a tale filled with irony and pathos in all this, a tale of well-intended gestures, hapless victims, maudlin sentiment. But it's not the tale I remember, or wish to reconstruct, though there are pictures and witnesses at my disposal. For me, the suffering of that day and that period in my family's life is summed up at the vanishing point in my own memory. And what I remember, finally, of that day, are Caroline's grasp—a warning, a reassurance, a commiseration—and how my grandfather's eyes, filled with pain, matched his pajamas and the roses on the cake and the burn of the sunlight through the drawn shades.

Second Sight

On the morning of September 11, 2001, while repairing a broken shower nozzle, Bradley Smith foresaw the death of his older brother, Darin, in an automobile accident on route 74 near Laurinburg, NC. Stunned, as if he'd seen a commercial jet fly into the World Trade Center, Bradley dropped his monkey wrench, cracking a bathroom tile.

A 38-year-old father and third-shift mechanic at a mill in Beckley, West Virginia, Bradley had arrived home earlier that morning to find that his wife, Krystal, and his three daughters were bleary-eyed, sullen, and disheveled. Only Colleen, his youngest, had managed a shower before the aged Water Pik shower head had broken clean of the stem, making morning ablutions impossible for the rest of the family. Colleen had already been out digging worms for her class terrarium and had therefore been the most in need of a bath, but at six years old she was also the least concerned about her appearance. Linda and Louise, eighth graders, were deeply troubled about going to school unclean and were convinced that despite heroic efforts with perfume and clothing, they would be sniffed out on the bus ride. "Everyone's so close together and Colleen tells everything." They were swearing Colleen to secrecy with threats to her life as Bradley walked through the door. Krystal greeted him with, "The shower's busted. I want it fixed by noon," at which point she planned to use her lunch hour at Dr. Caddy's office to rush home and clean up.

So it was that at 8:00, Bradley saw his girls out the door, wolfed down three Pop Tarts and a Pepsi, and turned up the *Today Show* loud enough that he could hear it in the bathroom. Bradley was struggling to dislodge a rusted coupling when he had his premonition.

Bradley saw Darin driving far too fast in his black Jeep, top off, down the highway. His radio blared the Marshall Tucker Band over the wind and the whine of his tires. A deer pranced out of the endless pines. Darin had no time to swerve. His Jeep mounted the deer, caught air, and flipped end over end down an embankment.

The monkey wrench slipped, clanged, and created a craquelure of gray in one of the black tiles that Bradley had laid in the bathroom just last June.

Recall your most unsettling nightmare. Now imagine that you'd been fully awake as the nightmare unfolded, a daydream of nightmare intensity, combined with the double perspective of being inside and outside the dream. You are aware of your dreaming and yet entangled in it, and while mere seconds pass, they seem like hours. Such was Bradley's experience of second sight, if we might call it that.

Bradley sat on the edge of the tub, his heart pounding so that he felt he had to hang on to prevent tipping over. He checked his watch: 8:15. Darin would have left for work by now. "I should call him," he thought, but didn't move. Katie Couric and her guests were laughing. The faucet burbled and dripped. Bradley breathed as if he'd run up a flight of stairs.

"Should I phone him?" he asked the cracked tile.

He and Darin had talked over the weekend. Darin would be hauling freight to Charleston on Thursday and figured he'd stay through Sunday. The two had planned to slip down to the lake on Saturday and fish. It was something they hadn't done in many years, since Bradley married and moved away. The distance between their homes, along with Bradley's nocturnal patterns and Darin's trucking, made visits impractical. When they talked, they tended to dream up escapes into the wilderness that both knew they'd never make happen. It was difficult enough to pick up the phone. Darin's call last Saturday had been unusual, there being no holiday to prompt it. "What the hell would I say if I phoned him?" Bradley thought, still staring at the tile, " 'Pull over, I've got ESP and you're about to crash?' He'll think I'm drunk before breakfast."

But no sooner had he mumbled these words than the terror which had shaken him just moments before returned. A radio blasted, tires squealed, and there was the body of his brother twisted in metal. Bradley darted to the phone. He began dialing Darin's cell, then stopped himself short of the last digits. "I'm losing it," he mumbled and hung up. His breath slowed, and he returned to his perch on the edge of the tub.

Bradley replayed this scene several times during the next forty minutes, back and forth between phone and tub.

On his final trip, he paused in front of the bathroom mirror. "This happened in a movie," he thought, for Bradley had been a movie junkie of sorts since he and Krystal had purchased satellite TV last Christmas. After the Today show, he would fall asleep watching whatever movie he landed on first while flipping through the channels. That was his policy: whatever he landed on first. He was indecisive otherwise and always hated what he chose after surfing endlessly. This way, it was just fate. And right now he'd swear that his experience of the last 40 minutes, up to and including his pausing before the mirror, had happened in a movie. He just couldn't say which movie. He never remembered titles.

He removed his cap and tried in vain to comb out the ring it had made in his black hair. His moustache was going grey—Krystal liked to point this out and laugh, because she still looked 21. He didn't mind. Aging didn't concern him, but he wondered about Darin. His older brother had never married and didn't have any children. That didn't seem to bother him. Though there was that day before the wedding when the two of them went bass fishing on the Pee Dee, and Darin said it would be strange to always wake up with the same person. "I don't mean in a bad way 'strange,'" he added, before Bradley could protest. "I mean, different. To always know what's coming next."

Bradley saw himself again in the mirror and felt the swirling disequilibrium of the jeep hurling end over end. He stumbled backwards into the bathroom door, steadied himself, got his bearings, and made once again for the phone.

It was then that an NBC news anchor interrupted regular programming to report that a plane had hit the World Trade Center. Bradley hung up the phone without dialing and sat on the couch in front of the big screen TV.

He was still there when Krystal arrived at 12:05. She sat down close to Bradley. She was trembling. Her eyes were bloodshot from crying, her makeup patchy and corrugated from hasty reapplications. She had spent the morning trying to manage Dr. Caddy's waiting room, which had assumed the atmosphere of a wake, mourners gathered around the television watching the planes fly repeatedly into the towers, much as she and Bradley watched now. "I kept trying so hard not to cry, because everybody in the office was falling apart," Krystal said, speaking for the first time since coming home. Bradley put a hand on her knee. "It didn't help that old Mrs. Henke, who's such a paranoid anyway, kept going on and on about what horrible deaths those people were dying…"

"There's no use in thinking about that kind of thing," Bradley quickly cut in.

"I know, but she'd say, 'They're burning to death. They're having to watch the flames getting closer and closer that's going to kill them.'"

"What's the use in thinking like that?" Bradley asked impatiently. Over and over he'd seen the planes hit the towers, but only now did he begin to imagine a person on fire.

"So I tried to calm her, that went nowhere, finally I had to say 'Mrs. Henke, it's hard enough without your describing it,' which pissed her off. But for Christ's sake, there were children in the office." Krystal's voice broke, and she began to shake.

Bradley stroked her hair, pushed it back and kissed her forehead. She cried for several minutes, and he kept stroking her hair and trying to stay focused on her while the towers burned in the background. As her sobbing softened, she ran her hands over his shoulders and pulled herself onto his lap, straddling his thighs.

It had been a long time since they'd had sex spontaneously, so long that Bradley was hesitant, waiting for a clearer signal of Krystal's intent. Why would it come now? He placed his hands on her waist and tried to read her, though his eyes kept drifting back to the smoke and plummeting bodies on the television. "I can't keep thinking about it," Krystal said and lifted up on her knees, blocking his view. She didn't look at him but quickly removed her taupe blouse.

Bradley was unhooking her bra when the phone rang. "It could be the girls," she announced, slipping out of his arms and over to the phone. She was right. Louise was calling from the cafeteria. She was in tears. Bradley tried not to resent the interruption. Wasn't this what happened in the movies? His readiness withered quickly at the renewed sounds of devastation from the Pentagon and New York City. He could have turned the TV off, the remote was within reach, but to do so seemed wrong.

Krystal hung up the phone and returned to Bradley's lap. She slid her hands into his trousers. "I'm sorry honey," she apologized. "I just couldn't not get the phone. I *knew* it was one of the girls."

In the end, the interruption proved as inconsequential as the newscast. The sex was good. Afterwards, as Krystal reluctantly acknowledged the approaching hour of her return to the office and slid off of Bradley in order to get dressed, the phone rang again. The lovers ignored it, having turned to the television. Silent, ashen-faced people were walking through an unnatural fog down Manhattan streets that neither Bradley nor Krystal would ever know, though both had the uncanny experience of recognizing someone in the crowd.

The answering machine picked up. It was Bradley's mother.

Bradley immediately assumed that she was phoning to witness to what had already been named, "Attack on America," the TV news having brought to the morning's events the comforting clarity of a story with a title. But soon after "it's mother" issued from the echo chamber of the machine, Bradley's premonition resurfaced, breaking through the Sony TV screen that had obfuscated it, such that as his mother wept, "has been killed in a car accident," Bradley watched once more that awful event which the "Attack on America" had preempted.

Bradley and Krystal agreed to take the smaller roads, avoiding the high speed and highways on the long drive to Laurinburg. The only conversation in the minivan that afternoon came from radio personalities and their callers, an endless exchange of bafflement and righteous anger, interspersed with periodic returns to the newsroom for retellings of the morning's events. When one station would fade, Krystal easily found another with similar content. Colleen slept. Linda and Louise, staring out the windows, were boxed in by familial and national tragedy and wondered, secretly, how long all this would take. It was only 7:30, but Bradley fought sleep. He had now been awake for 36 hours, hounded by regret to the point of exhaustion for the past six. "I should have phoned," he told himself repeatedly.

To stay awake, he tried noticing things along the road. He counted the houses with pampas grass by the driveway, but the numbers came so thick and fast that he gave up. He read the homespun aphorisms on church marquees: "Know Jesus, Know Life, No Jesus, No Life"; "You Can Tell A Christian By The Color Of His Bible—Always Read." But they all sounded the same, like "Attack on America," and in their certainty served mainly to remind him that he should have called. Hadn't he seen it coming?

His eyes began to glaze over. He needed coffee. At the next opportunity, Bradley pulled into a small service station—the Austin Gas n Go. It was country in quotation marks: a porch with rockers, flowers planted in milk cans, "welcum" painted on a wooden slab sign at the entrance, "ya'll come back" at the exit. Inside, a small group of men in overalls contributed to the ambience. They were gathered to watch lower Manhattan burn on the television perched on top of the store's freshly painted pot belly stove.

Bradley chose the largest styrofoam cup available and filled it with scorched coffee. One of the men left his seat by the stove to ring up the purchase. He was the only capless one, the store's owner.

"That'll keep you up!" he assured Bradley. "Been sitting there all afternoon."

Bradley fished in his pocket for change. "Yes, well, I was glued to the set, too, till I got on the road."

The owner laughed. "Oh, I was meaning the coffee's been sitting, but we ain't moved much neither. Can you believe that mess? Whole thing's so strange, like those alien invasion movies you used to see at the drive-in. But I reckon that was before your time."

"No, I know what you mean." Bradley looked over his shoulder at the screen. A fireman was being interviewed. He was crying.

The owner, suddenly angry, continued. "I mean, flying jets into skyscrapers…what kind of twisted bastards—pardon my French—could dream up such a thing? And they had to study on it, you know they did. Plan it for months and months. How come nobody caught on to them? Somebody must have known…FBI, CIA, what the hell—if you'll excuse the expression—what the hell do we pay those bastards to do? Don't you think somebody could've saw it coming?"

Bradley watched the camera pan to the smoldering towers. "It was just too strange, like you said. You can't see that kind of thing coming. If you did, you wouldn't believe it."

"I don't know. Somebody knew. That's how it always

turns out. Somebody knew, but somebody else had him by the short hairs so he kept his mouth shut. Like FDR knew about Pearl Harbor. Like half the Pentagon knew about Kennedy. I'd hate to be the bastard who didn't speak up about this thing, though. How could you sleep?"

Bradley nodded. How could you sleep, he wondered, gazing into his coffee. How could you sleep knowing you had seen it coming?

The cowbell on the entrance clanged, and Krystal stepped in. "Bradley, you almost finished? I'm only getting your mother's answering machine and I've said we'll be there by 8:30."

"Ma'am, it's my fault," the owner apologized. "He's been listening to me preach about this mess in New York City. You be off, son. Keep it on the right side of the yellow lines."

Bradley said nothing. But his eyes had widened, and he had begun to tremble. Weeks later, recalling this moment, Bradley could actually name the movie it came from: *It's a Wonderful Life*, when George Bailey realizes that his wish has been granted and that he has never been born. Terrified, astonished, George slowly turns to the camera. Bradley turned to Krystal.

"I saw it coming, Krystal. The whole thing."

Krystal suddenly receded and the store filled with dust and smoke. Tires screeched, there was a chorus of screams. Bradley's eyes began to sting and swell with tears. His grip tightened on the coffee, too tight; the boiling liquid gushed over his hands and down his arms.

Krystal gasped. The owner ran for a mop. "Ma'am, is he okay? I didn't mean to upset nobody."

"It's his brother," Krystal replied as she grabbed Bradley to keep him from toppling over. "He was killed this morning…"

"Krystal, I saw it coming, the whole thing."

Now the owner's jaw dropped and eyes widened. "Dear Lord, son, I had no idea you had a brother killed by them bastards in that mess. Was he in New York, or did he work at the Pentagon? I am so, so sorry I went on like that."

One of the men in overalls had come over to help steady Bradley. "Yes, son, you can't listen to Jim. We love him but he ain't one to think before he speaks."

Krystal shook her head, "No, his brother wasn't in…"

"Krystal," Bradley cried, cutting her off, "Maybe I could have stopped it. With a phone call."

"Bradley, what are you talking about? You need to calm down, honey. Nobody could have stopped it."

"That's right, son. Nobody could've seen this coming. Like you said, it's just too outrageous to believe. Forget what I said. I talk too goddamn…pardon, too much. I'm so sorry about your brother…"

Bradley turned in the direction of the store owner's voice. Through the thickening haze, he could not see the man, but could easily make out the iridescent glow of the television and the image, once again, of a jet making for its target. He shut out the voices of the men and Krystal, who was clearing up the confusion and apologizing for the mess. The jet was preternaturally silent, the sky far too blue. Then there was the noiseless crash. Had he not foreseen all of this? Hadn't this been the meaning of the premonition? He had been granted the gift of second sight. He had seen it coming. The whole thing. But what could he have done?

Krystal took over the driving and encouraged Bradley to rest, for he had to be strong and calm for his mother. With good reason, Krystal was filled with dread. Mrs. Smith forecast doom even during days of abundant health and cloudless serenity. Today affirmed her lifetime of pessimism, and Krystal anticipated an evening of oracular hysteria that only Bradley could calm. It was his gift in the family, soothing his mother. His method, if it could be called a method, was simple. Bradley went about his business, periodically smiling at his mother, and that was that. At Mrs. Smith's, his "business" usually consisted of home repairs or upgrades that had lain fallow since his father's death. He could grout the tub or change the furnace filter while his mother enumerated the signs of the times. Krystal wasn't sure he actually listened to his mother, but that didn't seem to matter. Bradley always emerged unscathed; Mrs. Smith, appeased.

"Your mother will need to talk at you, Bradley," she reminded him as he stared blankly at the glove compartment. "Think about what you can fix. It'll settle your mind a bit."

Krystal's suggestion had its intended effect. He thought about the fuse box at his mother's house. He tried to predict which outlets or appliances she'd lived without until he came again to replace the dead fuses. He then remembered the shower at his own house. Had he managed to get the remains of the shower head pried off? And what of that splintered tile? It would be no simple task to chip out the fragments and replace the tile without the scars of the repair being obvious. Formulating a plan occupied his mind until Krystal pulled the minivan into his mother's driveway. The floodlights flickered on, revealing the shambles of Darin's jeep, which had been towed onto the front lawn.

The lights also revealed Darin. He was on the porch having a cigarette. His head was bandaged, and his left arm was in a sling. He put up a hand to greet them.

Bradley gasped, closed his eyes, looked again. Yes, it was Darin. Alive. He turned to Krystal. She was gaping. "What the hell is going on?" she exclaimed. Bradley sat in stunned silence. They both did for another moment before Krystal's eyes narrowed. "Jesus Christ, Bradley, your mother really is a case."

Bradley continued to stare in amazement at his brother in the full artificial light of his mother's driveway. "What do you mean?"

"I mean she was hysterical when we talked to her at lunch. It's like everything with her—she'd convinced herself of the worst. Jesus!"

Bradley shook his head. "I don't know, Krystal, maybe she…"

Furious, Krystal interrupted him. "Don't make excuses for her. I can't believe what she's put us through. Of course, who knows, she's probably given herself a heart attack. Or she's wandering around the hospital still convinced he's dead. That woman's a basket case."

Bradley shook his head again. He had yet to take his eyes off his brother. "No. I don't think that's it, Krystal. She wouldn't have called us unless she knew."

"Well, no," Krystal was sardonic, "I guess maybe Darin has risen from the fucking dead!"

Bradley didn't respond. This isn't what he'd foreseen, thank God. If he had phoned, would that have made it worse? Maybe the distraction, the cell phone…maybe Darin would have had less control of the jeep. Bradley left Krystal and rushed up to his brother, who stepped back cautiously. "Slow down, man. I'm pretty sore. They wanted to keep me but I said hell no."

Darin's porch-light halo was flecked with moths. He smelled of sweat and iodine and menthol cigarettes. His beard had been shaved so that a gash on his chin could be stitched. His face looked smaller, childlike in its smooth pallor, but he still managed to affect his aloof, older-brother air.

Bradley was trembling. He finally managed to stammer, "Darin, I thought sure you were…I mean, Mama called and said…"

"Yeah, well, Mama's still hysterical. I've got a nurse in there with her right now. Woman's going to give herself a heart attack."

Now Krystal and the girls joined Bradley in the twilight just outside Darin's halo. Krystal was seething, but she felt no malice towards Darin. She moved forward to hug him.

He dodged her.

"I'm too sore, Kris."

Colleen, drool-matted hair clinging to her cheek like algae, worked her arms around Bradley's legs before asking Darin if he'd seen a bright light.

"What you mean honey?"

"She's thinking of them second chance shows," Linda explained. "You know, when somebody near about dies but comes back having seen Jesus or an angel."

Darin chuckled, "Didn't see no angels, unless they're growing twelve-point racks."

"So it *was* a deer?" Bradley asked. He saw the jeep take air, he saw the planes smash into the towers.

"Came out of frigging nowhere," Darin cursed, lighting another cigarette. "I didn't even have time to swerve. Funny thing is that if I'd had my seatbelt buckled, they'd still be trying to pick pieces of me out of that scrap heap of a jeep. Instead I got flung clear of the wreck."

As if on cue, everyone turned to the demolished jeep. Bradley saw his brother twisted into the steering wheel. In the shattered windshield was the reflection of his mother's living room window, lit by the TV. She and her nurse sat in front of it.

"We stopped for coffee," Krystal said, poking her husband in the side as if to wake him, "and Bradley made quite a mess." Rolling her eyes, she rounded up the girls and headed inside.

Bradley noticed that Darin was offering him a cigarette. "Yeah, well, I was pretty shook up," he admitted, accepting a light. "And that guy, with his 'FBI should've seen this coming' bullshit. I mean, I know the government's crooked, but God himself couldn't see this coming."

"Oh hell no," Darin agreed. "But somebody will pay."

Bradley heard the clang of a hammer against ceramic. "Yeah, well you know, I was just about to call you this morning." He hesitated and took a drag on his cigarette.

"Why?"

"I thought I had a premonition. About your wreck."

"Yeah?" Darin said, the way he always had when he wasn't sure what to say. "Well, I walked away from it. Can't say as much for the frigging deer. So don't think too much about it."

Bradley nodded. "Anyway, I'm glad Mama was wrong." He reached out to lay a hand on Darin's shoulder. Darin pulled back.

Inside the TV chattered faintly. Bradley cleared his throat.

"Busted your casting arm?"

"Yeah."

"Reckon we'll have to take a rain check on that lake getaway."

"Reckon so."

Bradley shrugged and gazed down the street. In every house, windows glowed blue while televisions showed a plane hit a tower again and again and again.

To the Falls

I came upon a flock of cedar waxwings in a hemlock grove. The grove edged a creek I was following to where it had long ago burst a neglected dam and generated a waterfall, frozen now in mid-February. The waterfall was my destination, but I paused to listen to the birds. A waxwing's song does not dazzle though it brims with cheer, the kind that Charles Dickens attributes to Fezziwig at his Christmas dance, his calves shimmering as he cuts a figure. Roger Tory Peterson writes of waxwings that they are "gregarious" and "often indulge in fly-catching." Winter enforces abstinence, and flies being scarce, my flock seemed satisfied with chirping and preening in the clean, cold sunlight.

The falls, as I mentioned, was the destination, though not as an end in itself, the way waterfalls tend to be. Samuel, who had recently turned eleven, was meeting his acting troupe to shoot a promotional photograph for their upcoming production of Shakespeare's *Henry V*. The photo was to be a lean, black and gray affair, on the order of Trevor Nunn's staging of *Macbeth* or of a U2 album cover from the band's early, college-radio years. With hard stares away from the camera and each other, the brooding preteens would be backed by sublime arctic harshness.

Months before, in the November rains, an oak had lost its hold on the creek bank and collapsed into the falls. Now having accumulated several weeks of freezing spray and snow, the oak had become the main beam of a gothic ice castle, rough and ruinous. It might have belonged to the emperor of the moon, in the times before we learned that the moon is lifeless (though now that water has been discovered, there is renewed scope for the imagination.) It was an astonishing accident of time and weather.

"The passion caused by the great and sublime in nature," writes Edmund Burke, "when those causes operate most powerfully, is astonishment; and astonishment is that state of the soul in which all its motions are suspended, with some degree of horror." To be astonished is, literally, to be thunderstruck, for the Latin "tonare" rumbles in the belly of the word. Burke goes on to explain that the sublime object so fills our mind that reason is bypassed. If it sometimes precedes curiosity, astonishment always precludes skepticism. This accounts for the connection between coming upon a waterfall and, say, confronting a ghost. Were we astonished by the ice falls? Though we knew a frozen waterfall was around the bend, and "horror" was unlikely since we were not in a canoe careening toward the edge, there was real wonder, if only momentarily. For the troop of young actors was soon considering how the structure was made. They were investigating the architecture, analyzing its design, and testing its stability. Kids climbed the main beam, daring it to shift, and crept along ice floors until cracks began forming. Reconnaissance of this kind muffles the thunder, which is after all a mere side effect of lightning, itself simply a spark. Above the falls, the waxwings chatted.

While winter had augmented the visual drama of the scene, it had done so by bridling the water's boisterous energies, by taming and silencing the falls. I shift metaphors because sound normally factors in astonishment, and a raging falls is a thundering of hooves, horses driving towards the precipice and over it. Both embody overwhelming power. Burke recalls an image from the Book of Job, when out of a whirlwind God challenges his beleaguered servant and declares his sovereignty as creator. Of the horse, God declares, "hast thou clothed his neck with thunder?...He swalloweth the ground with fierceness and rage." The sheer amplitude of the falls swallows up other sounds. When you call out, it is as if your voice fractures as it leaves you. Enfeebled, thinned, it crumples under the water's volume.

I learned this painfully one summer on a hike with my father and my two sons, then six and eight years old. The boys scampered ahead of us and quickly scaled the mossy rock face by a tiered waterfall in the Catskill Mountains. "Couple of little billy goats," my father joked, and when they vanished over the top, he tried not to appear worried. Not wanting to leave him behind or force him to climb too fast, I laughed in response and called for the boys to wait. My voice disappeared into the pounding of the waters.

If God on that day had been mercifully inclined, she might have blown a northern breath, locking the stampede in ice in midsummer, so my sons could hear me. Jacob, the youngest and usually the least cautious, reappeared, surprisingly, the energy of his forward motion having converted to fear when he lost sight of Samuel. He stopped in a glen, an echo chamber for the waterfall, such that even his desperate cries of "Sammy, Sammy" had no lift as his brother left him behind. I handed Jacob to my father, commanded both of them to stay put, and set out in search of Samuel.

I assumed that he would follow the creek and that if I ran, surely I would catch up to him. The banks were marshy, hiding vines and fallen branches. What if Sammy had tripped and hit his head on a stone? In similar circumstances my great uncle, Fordham, had drowned. He was a farmer. His cows had been turning up along the road and in fields, so Fordham was walking the fence line in search of a break. In sections, the fence bordered a creek, which was swollen and swift with the late April rain. Fordham must have waded in where the line had been overtaken by the waters. He was a strong man and by all accounts a superb swimmer, but a shrapnel wound made his left leg prone to cramps. Whether he became tangled in flooded brush and barbed wire, or his leg seized up, or he fell and struck his head, or some combination of these was left to speculation and the storyteller's discretion. But those were pearls that were his eyes. And his body was discovered on Mother's Day.

The roar of the falls diminished as I ran up the creek, and my shouts finally received a reply. I ran faster. A child's voice in such emotionally fraught contexts redoubles the urge to secure and protect. The only sound I could hear, despite the distant stampede, was Sammy's cry. He later told me that he had been looking for the source of the creek, something I had suggested we do together, though Sammy became excited about being the discoverer. Astonishment at the waterfall had given way to curiosity, which can be simultaneously rational and reckless. One moves from being overwhelmed to being in a state of focused oblivion. The truth is that Sammy had not become afraid until he heard my voice, and then not because he feared punishment, for like most parents in such a situation, I was too relieved to exact consequences. Rather, he hadn't thought to be afraid while he doggedly followed the creek. He was surprised by how far he had come, unawares and unafraid. He had the same reaction on the day of the Shakespeare photo shoot when he went missing beyond the falls and I found him. Having lost interest in the ice castle, he had set out to locate where, precisely, the creek began to freeze. I intercepted him beneath the cedars filled with waxwings.

We go to a waterfall to be thunderstruck. Even in this most cynical of ages, we want to believe that astonishment is possible, like true love, and waterfalls of all kinds are putatively astonishing. Niagara is likely the image that leaps first to mind for many of us at the mention of "waterfall," a trysting place, in which the falls themselves disappear in the snow globe storm of honeymoon clichés. Plunging waters invoke the drama of eros, the exposure and the ecstasy, while the sound, in contrast, envelopes the newly-weds, offering a mode of privacy, a blanket. Like love, the waterfall seems to demand poetry even as it tests the limits of original expression and description. For a waterfall is a poeticized space, a setting and an emblem, and descriptive lyrics about a falls constitute a small, peculiar subgenre of topographical writing, tucked away within bigger projects or oeuvres. Astonishment is often their subject, but rarely their method or their exclusive focus. They draw our attention to the fact that to visit a falls is to hear poetry as well as the plunge, to write about one is to confront literary history as well as a natural phenomenon.

Thomas Hardy's contribution to the kind, "Under the Waterfall," published just before the First World War, is a case in point. In the poem, a woman tells her companion about a "little valley fall" beside which she and a former lover once shared a "basket of fruit and wine." The poem is a dialogue, though the reminiscing woman dominates, and we have the impression that it takes place over a dish-pan, for she claims that she recalls the "purl" of the falls whenever she plunges her arm into a basin of cold water, as she does now. That tranquil purl is amplified to a "hollow boiling voice" later in the stanza, in much the same way that a "feeble brook" in the Ravine of Arve takes on a grander, more intense music as it courses toward a precipice in Percy Shelley's "Mont Blanc." Rapids pace Shelley's poem and supply its energy, but for Hardy's speaker, the sound of the falls follows from the sensation of cold water against flesh, part of a circuit that ends by conjuring her lone image of romantic bliss. The process of association through which the speaker recollects emotion is complex—from touch through sound to sight—and therefore rings true, but her companion by the dishpan wonders, as do we, why icy water evokes romance.

Wedged between stones under the falls is a drinking glass, she explains, the very glass from which she and her lover sipped wine together. Not that they had flung it into the falls, post-quaff. Rather, it tumbled from her hand as she rinsed it, the aftermath of their momentary romantic indulgence requiring a pause, a breather, clean-up. The cheekiness here is mine, not Hardy's, but the irony of the woman's nostalgic tale turns out to be the poet's main interest. The lovers tried to retrieve their glass, they "plumbed that little abyss/ with long bared arm," but the glass was "past recall." Nostalgia depends on loss; the pleasures of memory collect in emptied spaces. Under the waterfall, "there lies intact that chalice of ours," the woman declares, effectively claiming abundant recompense for her losses, in that the drinking glass has become a chalice and the tryst a sacrament. It is of course significant that the glass did not break; it is her chastity, preserved by sinking out of reach. There, an ideal may remain "intact." From a less idealistic point of view—Hardy's, the reader's, maybe that of the woman's companion at the dishpan—romantic love in this tale has plunged deep beneath the falls, beneath the hollow din and frigid waters. It is inaccessible. I imagine the woman's companion, who speaks only to ask pointedly skeptical questions, to be a Hardy man, time's laughingstock, Jude Fawley or Clym Yeobright, an idealist doomed, ironically, by the ideals of his beloved.

You always arrive at a waterfall after someone else, someone whose words were almost yours. As in his more familiar "Darkling Thrush," Hardy doesn't share the emotional lift occasioned by his subject in "Under the Waterfall." To him, the waterfall is full of emptiness, of ideals in quotation marks, literally those of a woman whose nostalgia he rejects. It is so in large part because it is a literary waterfall, that is to say, nature transmitted and transformed through symbolic language, much as the thrush's song is an echo of the nightingales and larks that overrun the poetical landscape in all seasons. I mentioned that Hardy's "runlet" echoes Shelley's "feeble brook," and the intact chalice serves a similar purpose to an iris that Byron's Childe Harold spies next to a "matchless cataract," the Marmore waterfall. Like the drinking glass deep under Hardy's waterfall, the iris is a pure ideal, indestructible because unreachable. The flower "sits,

> …amidst the infernal surge,
> like Hope upon a death-bed, and, unworn
> Its steady eyes, while all around is torn
> By the distracted waters, bears severe
> Its brilliant hues with all their beams unshorn:
> Resembling, 'mid the torture of the scene,
> Love watching Madness with unalterable mien.

Love and hope both…the iris bears a heavy load, not unlike the feminine ideal it also symbolizes, countenancing the maddening, "horribly beautiful" falls that represent Harold's frenetic, impassioned life and tortured soul. Harold goes to the falls to be astonished, and he is, but only to have the value of astonishment called into question. In a footnote, Byron comments on the actual falls, ostensibly to defend his choice of Marmore among the many European falls he's seen. Pedantic and dismissive, the note has the effect of further ameliorating the sublime, for Byron will not fully submit to Harold's astonishment. The footnote brings a second order of self-consciousness to the passage, the first order being implicit in the elaborate metaphor Byron has developed to make his point about love's constancy and madness. Imagine Byron, as Harold, by the falls. The iris is an Astarte—a hallucination or, more favorably, a vision that Byron must include not only to ballast the falls' sublimity with the beautiful, but also to bring love (and his own biography) into the emblem. As a romantic, Byron would like to cling to both, the sublime and the beautiful. But as a skeptic, he would also lay claim to irony, the ability to step out of the dramatic scene for editorial commentary. Now imagine Hardy looking over Byron's shoulder. He sees Harold (or is that Byron in disguise?), and the steadfast, delicate iris. His irony is more direct than Byron's because his skepticism is deeper seated. His falls might dislodge a boulder to crush that flower, if flower there really was. An ideal can only be allowed to continue if we present it as merely that—as fantastic, as wish-fulfillment. At the very least, I imagine Hardy would place Harold's observations in quotation marks and thereby maintain, if only symbolically, the distance between poet and speaker that Byron famously disowned when he published the final cantos.

Hardy knew Shelley and Byron's falls, but the waterfall that looms largest for his poem is Henry Vaughan's, composed in the mid-17th century. The first stanza of Vaughan's waterfall, alternating pentameter and trimeter lines, actually looks like a series of cascades before the steady flow of the remaining stanzas, and Hardy roughly imitates the look and the metric in two stanzas of his own waterfall poem. However, for Vaughan, the brook and falls provide an allegory for human passage through life to eternity. Time carries us toward a precipice, as water tumbles toward the cliff's edge. Vaughan observes the swell of water near the "steep place" and imagines us drawing back as time pulls us closer to death. But if going over the falls signals an end of our meandering journey through this world, the mists rising from the pools below are human spirits returning to paradise. "But quick'ned by this deep and rocky grave," he writes, souls, like the spray from the plunge, "Rise to a longer course more bright and brave." The water cycle—the idea of water passing through its various states—nourishes Vaughan's recondite Christian poetics more than the falls themselves. "O useful Element and clear!" he declares, invoking water's status among the four elements of creation and, more importantly to Vaughan, in the sacrament of baptism, washing sin away.

He prefers the "deep murmurs" of the brook to the cataract's turbulence that would later enthrall Childe Harold. The quieter voice is not simply reassuring but more persuasive than the bombast of cascading water. It whispers of an "invisible estate" in the mists above and beyond the falls.

It is significant that while Vaughan ostensibly sits by the falls, Harold stands before them, and Hardy's speaker is transported to them by a process of association, each ends up drawing our attention away from the dramatic spectacle and towards something smaller, more delicate, and more significant. Differences in sensibility and historical period do not seem to alter the fundamental pattern. Hardy's falls grow louder, Byron's softer, but in none does the thunder or deep murmur provide the language that proves most necessary to the poet, even though the setting is essential to the poet's insight. In W. S. Merwin's "Hearing," from *Opening the Hand* (1983), neither the waterfall nor any idea of it enters the poem until the fourth stanza, but it is only after becoming fully involved with the falls that the poet has the experience that gives the poem its title. Although the poem is brief, the pace is slow, and the diction precise and quiet. Merwin begins on a marshy plain, travels slowly through a village into the foothills, then trains our eyes on the "inky forests" situated between the cloudy mountaintops and "airy valleys" below. As we ascend, a waterfall appears, and it is now that we learn the poet has a companion. The mist from the falls "drifted/around us," he recalls, and "swirling into the broad leaves/

and the waiting boughs," it knits poet and companion into the forest. Merwin climbs the rocks and branches by the waterfall in order to fill a tin cup with water. The upward movement here is important; his surroundings are paradisiacal. Although we have already heard the thundering of the falls, the more important "hearing" is yet to come. The poet reaches his cup towards the falls, and from under his right foot, on a stone in deep water, "came a voice like a small bell singing/ over and over one clear treble/ syllable." The voice moves through the poet's body, like an electrical current, and he hears with all his senses. When he drinks the water, for instance, the voice "rang in my eyes," and this continues even after he descends to share another cup with his companion. This is astonishment of the kind described by Burke, but it is brought on not by the thunder but by a small voice under the water. Astonishment gives rise to synesthesia, which in turn distributes the power of the experience over the entire body.

Although the poem is set in a tropical climate (there are jacanas in the first stanza) and evidences Merwin's interest in Asian poetries and Zen Buddhism, the experience in "Hearing" is closely analogous to Vaughan's in "The Waterfall." It is about contact with an "invisible estate"—contact that is sensual and, incongruously, extra-sensory, in that it registers between and beyond the normal bounds of sensation. This is not astonishment but wonder, a kindred sensation and less evanescent. Unlike Vaughan, Merwin does not begin his poem as an argument for belief or faith. In fact, in this small group of poetic waterfalls, Merwin's offers, up to a point, the purest description of topography, with Byron running a close second. But I say "up to a point" because in its wonder, "Hearing" is arguably the most transcendent, if least heavy-handed, of these poems. In a mode of communion that transcends that taken by Hardy's speaker, Merwin and his companion drink "the light water," a water infused with sun and conducive to a lightness of being. The drinking, in fact, takes place after the ecstatic experience has begun. Even as the poet reaches to fill his cup, one has the impression that he hovers, or almost hovers, since his foot touches down on the stone from which the voice emanates. While gods sometimes speak in still, small voices, Merwin never names the voice or rationalizes it in any way. We only know that a pilgrimage to the falls seems to have been necessary to hearing it.

Even if we could disperse the mists of symbolic language that have gathered between us and the waterfall, if we could, as William Carlos Williams declares in *Paterson*, "strike in" through the waters and come back with some "well packed clause," original and exact, only poetry would prove sufficient—or approximately sufficient—to the task of representing the place and our experience of it. Poets have the urge to make it new, to astonish, but every poem is an echo, and in the falls we hear voices. Poetry demands that we attend to those voices, not simply to the pulsing of the cataract and of our heart. All water falls along the natural decline of the land, from the peaks to its lowest margins. The waterfall is an abrupt acceleration in this inexorable motion downward, a place of energy and high drama. Such moments are hard to follow, in life or in landscape. Nature is wisest. Just beyond the plunge, carried safely outward on concentric ripples, we end up in a quiescent pool. The splash and roar dull our senses if we linger, hoping to sustain astonishment, which is inherently unsustainable. The falls are for a moment only. The iris, the brook, the glass of light, these are what we must actually hold to. Steadiness sustains us—a whisper, not a roar, keeps our attention. The latter becomes white noise after an initial shock, whereas we never cease straining to make sense of the still small voice.

My office building is perched near the edge of a waterfall. Originally the home of a professor of religion, a Mr. Shafer, whose name the office now bears, it was built for the view. An array of large plate glass windows and balconies affords spectacular scenery of the Saw Kill in all seasons, and makes the building impossible to heat in the bitter winters of the Hudson Valley. Except when the river freezes between January and March, reducing the flow to a narrow ribbon of green water, the roar of the falls provides theme music for the dramas of our workplace. Not that we are a theatre group, or that we experience the high drama of a hospital ER. By the Saw Kill falls, Shafer houses a fledgling teacher education program with grand ideas for changing public schools. Because schools refuse to reform quickly, and reformers refuse to move slowly, most of our agitation and angst could be classed with adventure melodrama, a birch bark canoe careening towards the swell, villain and hero locked in combat. The sound of the billowing cascade is the arpeggios in the pianist's left hand.

However, most of our work is less stage-worthy: analysis and planning, thinking, writing and revising, negotiation and mediation, the modes of a teacher and scholar. Under the circumstances, the waterfall, despite its pomp and glory, is quotidian, a backdrop. It moves to the foreground when a prospective student or employee arrives and, invariably, remarks enviously upon the beauty of our setting. And it forces itself into our consciousness in the spring, when the Catskill snows begin to melt and the river floods. Raging waters have, on more than one occasion, fully surrounded the building, creating a turbulent moat. Safety inspectors are called out, and we stare at the spectacle, speculating about whether this year the foundation will crumble and our little enterprise will tip over the falls.

That perspective, bearing down on the cliff's edge, is only melodramatic if you're not in the canoe, as it sometimes feels we are in Shafer, especially in April. We grow accustomed to the falls, then it suddenly threatens to overwhelm us, and we're all paddling furiously in the opposite direction. Natty Bumpo, the insufferably bardic frontiersman also known as Hawkeye in James Fenimore Cooper's Leatherstocking Tales, offers a different solution. He successfully shoots the Oswego falls in a canoe with his protégé Eau Douce, the two setting a standard for subsequent woodland adventures and wild-west tales. This climactic scene happens early in *The Pathfinder*, so the bar is high for Bumpo's remaining exploits. We no longer read Cooper for pleasure or instruction. Clichés are recognized from above, and Cooper now appears to be beneath us. But if we suspend our contemporary predilection for irony, Hawkeye's example is as thrilling as it is implausible. While I would never suggest that we send Shafer downstream, there is sometimes nothing for it but to brace and plunge.

Once more unto the breach. While the young King Henry's St. Crispin's Day speech is sublime, I prefer the quiet beauty of the field of campfires through which the hero wanders in disguise, gauging the humors of his men on the night before battle. As Sammy and his company broke off from their still life and became real children again, they gallivanted in pairs and trios back through the woods, the frozen falls quickly receding. In time, what if anything will they make of their trip to the ice falls? There will be an elegant photo, black and white, the light sheering in every direction from the ice behind them. The falls will hold them all within its ambit. Yet today was merely a prelude, the falls a background. The play's the thing.

Courante (To him my tale I teach)

Paddling Miss Patsy

Third grade was a watershed year in my romantic life. Disillusioned with the girls in my class—that assortment of Barbie collectors and Shaun Cassidy worshippers who'd taken my chocolate but rejected my overtures the year before—I went in search of a higher ideal and found it in my teacher, Miss Patsy. Handsome, clever, and rich with youthfulness, she spoke to us in an authentic, raspy voice—none of your treacly second-grade-teacher "now honey" from her. She snorted loudly when she laughed. She wore jeans, chewed gum, and played kickball. Her green eyes, distorted behind her glasses, were nothing like the sun. But she winked at us often, and mussed our hair almost daily.

Determined to help us on our way towards becoming good citizens and passable scholars, she was constantly on the lookout for charitable acts and efforts at self-improvement. She gave me a Mary Jane candy once for trying to show my first-grade brother how to multiply. She gave Sandra Gillfilly two for thanklessly cleaning up everyone's paper scraps after book report collage making. Robbie Stoop rated a seat by her at lunch once he began to comb, regularly, his tangle of nit-ridden hair. She was quick to wrath, and mighty in it, when we were bad. But after she'd made her point, she loved us openly again. I was enthralled by Miss Patsy, and no doubt I was not alone.

Perhaps it was for this reason—the imminent threat of rival suitors—that I set about laying a claim upon her heart. I wrote her a love letter. It was in the late fall, the open windows of our classroom admitting a cool breeze laced with the fragrance of pine and poultry farms, and she was reading to us from a biography of Andrew Jackson. I was a devotee of presidential biographies—I was working my way through a series of them from our library: <u>Meet George Washington</u>, <u>Meet Thomas Jefferson</u>, <u>Meet Abraham Lincoln</u>—and I told her so in my note. *Who is your favorite president? I like Lincoln best.* After this casual opener, I confessed my longing to be her boyfriend. I remember scribbling my confession hurriedly: *I love you. Do you love me? Please check "yes"!*

I was too shy to deliver the note. Burying it among the multiplication worksheets in my desk, I spent the winter months searching out more indirect methods of expressing my devotion: washing the blackboard, carrying books to her car, sneaking parts of my Little Debbie snack cakes onto her desk, scribbling her initials in the margin of my worksheets. Paddling her.

I paddled Miss Patsy after our class birthday party for everyone born in March. We had these parties each month, on the last Friday, the climactic event after cake, song, and ice cream being the birthday paddling. Just before we left for the buses, Miss Patsy would dole out the licks with her paddle, on which she had painted a wincing, blonde boy with a bright red, bare behind. She staged the birthday licks dramatically. She made you bend over and grab your ankles. She inhaled loudly and reared back as she would before smacking a softball deep into left field. Then, with everyone holding his breath, she swung swiftly, only to catch herself up short and tap out the licks lightly. It was a ritual we all loved and dreaded simultaneously, the way you feel when you're next in line for a roller coaster. You're eager for the thrill, but uncertain about getting on.

A March baby, I got my licks that day along with my cousin, Polk. He was older than I by two weeks, so he went first in our line of two. Miss Patsy asked him to state his date and day of birth. Always precise and formal with adults, Polk answered, "Polk Clement Shinn, born 9 AM Sunday, March 8, 1968." Then, in unison with Miss Patsy, everyone chanted, "the child that's born on Sunday/ is bonny and blithe and good and gay." Polk grabbed his ankles, and we counted off the licks, one to nine.

I was born on a Monday afternoon, and I dreaded my line from the poem more than the actual licks: "Monday's child is fair of face." Only my mother could have claimed that I lived up to that promise. Near-sighted, buck-toothed, willowy, pale, and red-headed, I was as far from "fair of face" as Salt Lick, N.C. was from metropolitan. When everyone blared the line as I grabbed my ankles, I cringed and awkwardly tried to close my lips over my embarrassing overbite.

Moments later, the plot was hatched to paddle Miss Patsy. Polk and I were back at our desks when Mr. Mercer, the school principal, came to the door to speak to her. Troy Gray remarked that Miss Patsy's birthday had been in March, too, but we didn't know how old she was. Then Alfred Brewster jumped up from his chair and whispered frantically, "No one's gave her her licks yet!" There was a chorus of whispered "yeahs!" and giggles of shock at the mere suggestion, but without so much as a moment's reflection, I scampered quietly to the blackboard, retrieved the paddle from the hook where Miss Patsy had hung it, sidled along the wall out of Miss Patsy's line of peripheral vision, and planted myself firmly behind her, as if in the batter's box. *If anyone was going to make the bold gesture*, I thought, *it had better be he who loves her most.*

Why didn't Mr. Mercer stop me? A portly man with a carefully greased comb-over, dressed always in blue polyester suits and smelling of Mennen aftershave, Mr. Mercer's appearance belied his iron-fisted, Puritanical rule. He was Jonathan Edwards transported to the modern South, lecturing our grade school weekly on the slippery slope of slovenliness and poor hygiene. We had been in chapel just that morning, in fact ("chapel" didn't become "assembly" in our public school until well after my graduation). In a forty-five minute lecture, Mr. Mercer had traced for us the direct line from mumbling the Pledge of Allegiance—a sin that many of us had been guilty of minutes earlier—to unemployment, crime, and eternal damnation. Discipline was the pursuit of happiness. Lack of it bred suffering and shame, a point that Mr. Mercer brought home to Salt Lick School with his paddle.

That paddle hung by his office door, and to my eight-year-old eyes, looked like an oar. Those in the know, such as Shane Henson, who frequented Mercer's high office, warned that he had a veritable arsenal of specialized instruments of torture: paddles with holes drilled in them to make them swifter, paddles duct taped and re-taped after having been broken on the bums of naughty children, paddles with barbs made by carefully sharpened nails. In playground lore, his ferocity had earned him a nickname—from his Christian name, Ray, we had derived the "Razor Blade."

On Wednesdays, he paddled the week's arch-offenders —the fighters, back-talkers, class-sleepers and nose-pickers. They lined up along a wall outside his office, which was in the center of the school. When his swing made contact with butt, the smack crackled down the hall like a gunshot echo. I had occasion to be in the line once, innocently and inadvertently. In second grade, I broke my glasses at recess, and Miss Marsha sent me to the office for Super Glue. I didn't know the protocol for requesting glue, but I did know as a second grader that lines were to be waited in. So I did, and with each step I trembled more violently at the whacks, squeals, and whimpers that went before me. When my turn came, I found Mercer with his coat off and sleeves rolled up, paddle resting by his side like a Winchester rifle. Were there sweat beads on his brow? With evident exasperation, he remarked, "Your name's not on my list, young man, and

I'm surprised to see you here. What'd you do?" Did I faint at that point? Perhaps, because my next memory is of being back in class, glasses taped, clandestinely reading "Meet Martin Luther King, Jr." while Miss Marsha droned on about place value.

How was it, then, that he, whose very gaze could bring tears of penitence from a would-be delinquent, studiously ignored me as I prepared to whack my teacher with a paddle? It was as if he saw the harmless intent. He kept right on talking to Miss Patsy. Thus assured, and supported by the amazed stares of my humbled rivals, I swung. I swung hard. My heart was pounding and I let rip with a swing that, as soon as my elbows snapped, I realized was much harder than I intended. I gasped, but I was powerless to stop the motion. It was all physics now. Force A would travel surely along its trajectory until a greater or equal force B collided with it. And, alas, there was nothing but air between the paddle and Miss Patsy's blue-jeaned posterior.

Surely the smack must have reverberated down the long hall of our school. But I have no recollection, not so much as a sound-byte, of the noise at the moment of contact. I can feel the weight of the paddle and the jolt through my arms. I can see poor Miss Patsy, my beloved, pitch forward and catch herself on the door frame. There's no sound in all this before she whirls around and glares at me in astonishment. Had she had three snarling heads, fangs, and eyes of flame, she could not have been more terrifying to me than in that moment.

Then it was as if someone cranked up the volume. She

howled with anger and righteous indignation. "What are you doing, mister? What...what are you thinking?"

I couldn't speak. For brief moment, neither could Miss Patsy. She gasped, sputtered and glared. Then someone—was it Polk, Troy, or Alfred?—shouted "Birthday licks!"

It was as if he'd uncorked the bottle. Growing up Southern Baptist, I've been blasted into a pew more than once by the hot breath of a preacher whose fury at my sinfulness was mere dry wind next to the gale force of Miss Patsy's diatribe. "When have I hit you that hard? When have I ever sneaked up on you or anyone? That is unacceptable, completely unacceptable young man, and your mother will be hearing about it. Your father, too, I went to school with him, you know. What will he say, do you think? Hitting a teacher. I'm shocked. Why would you ever think it's okay to hit me at all?"

For minutes, her words rained down like hail but I stopped hearing them. I shriveled up white as a leper, her words pounding me like stones on Stephen.

I slunk back to my desk. I was choking with tears. *I hadn't meant to hit her hard*, I mumbled to no one. I really hadn't meant to *hit* anything, but my arms had just gotten away from me. I only did it because, well, I was the one who *should* give her the birthday licks, just as I was the one who should clean her erasers and carry her books to the car and wear her class ring when the time came. Anyone else would have been an imposter whose love for her could not possibly equal mine. Now, alas, I would have the dubious distinction of being the one who'd spanked his teacher, when in my heart of hearts, I just wanted to be her favorite.

Her screed continued until the bell, Mr. Mercer—arms crossed, face suddenly stern—nodding all the while. I didn't understand this, and still it seems incongruous to me. Why didn't he wrench the paddle from my hand, stand me on a desk, and make an example of me? I cannot now see him clearly enough to say with certainty. His legend looms in the way, and it is deflated by the explanation that I want to give, the one that humanizes him, says he sympathized. The quality of mercy is not strained, mused the Razor, who must have known something about swinging a paddle harder than he intended. Whatever the reason, he did not stop me as I scurried out, timorous as Robert Burns' mouse, to the bus. And though I lay awake that night expecting a trip to the principal and certain doom the next day, nothing came of it. After gathering her wits, Miss Patsy must have decided that my shame had been punishment enough. She must have connected the dots between my book-toting and paddle-swinging, and chosen to let it go. She never mentioned the paddling to me again, and with a typical nine-year-old's resiliency, I was back to courting her affections, clandestinely, within a week.

But at this point, I knew it was a lost cause. Somehow, that didn't matter. Winning her hand was no longer the goal. Rather I was learning to relish the pang of an impossible romance, and becoming skilled at the gestures—too dramatic or trite by turn—that fan its pallid embers.

Please Sit Up at Your Desk and Pay Attention

I
Simon, are you asleep?

"The dawn on bright stilts wades in from the shore," Czeslaw Milosz writes in the poem "Recovery." How many sunrises had Milosz observed before he noticed the stilts? Or how many aubades had he read and written, re-read and re-written, before the dawn arrived in this way? Outside our window, dawn arrives in Toyotas and garbage trucks. Having only recently become urban, I am awakened most mornings just before sunrise by the traffic on our street. On Saturdays, no one is racing to work, so the sound is almost soporific. The long inhale of an approaching car, the long exhale of its passing, is the breath of sleepers. A song sparrow in the roadside maple fills the space between. I move to my desk in the den, put on the radio, and add a sax duet by Warne Marsh and Ted Brown. This is my failing, spreading my attention too widely when there is no need, so I stop at three sounds. Multi-task became a verb, art went into decline. Close, sustained attention to mornings—poetic mornings, and those that precede the alarm clock—is what brings them on bright stilts.

"Blink if you're with me," my high school biology teacher said while explaining glycolysis. Imagine what he saw—twenty-six slouched teenagers, lolling heads, vacant stares. Teaching, you must hold their attention; learning, they must give it. Imagine a web of tightly stretched rubber bands, for inside "attention" is "attend," the root of which means "to stretch." Attention requires what Jane Austen called elasticity of mind; it also requires the will to be held taut. What prevents a student from snapping back and curling up in his desk chair? What prevents you, teacher, from letting go of your end?

Here is a familiar scene to a teacher. There is information that you must convey before your students can launch on their projects. You begin to hold forth, as enthusiastically as you know how, but nonetheless you feel several of those taut bands between you and the students sag. Lassitude is catching, so you say, "Give me your attention," or in a more demanding frame of mind, "Pay attention." Those are loaded phrases. Whether gift or payment, attention is costly. It takes work and time. "Just stay with me," you plead, because you know that in due time there will be abundant recompense. "The waiting," sings Tom Petty, "is the hardest part."

Recall being in the student's place. Attendance is required, and you must be an attendant of sorts, one who stands at attention and waits upon...what, in this case? First the content, then its meanings, which you'll only gather by holding to the content attentively—stretched, that is to say, at the ready. This is no thumb-twiddling waiting, en attendant Godot. Stretched, alert, ready to move: you would not be found sleeping. Jesus' pupils knocked off in the garden of Gethsemane while he prayed for clemency. Disappointed, he upbraided Simon Peter, "Simon, dormis? Non potuisti una hora vigilare?" *Simon, sleepest thou? Couldst thou not watch one hour?* The teacher appeals to guilt and expediency. *Is this the best you can do? You're here, now be vigilant.* My conscience says such things. *Your Latin is woefully inadequate. Don't put your head down on Wheelock's and expect to awaken with the declensions inscribed in your memory.*

Wait and watch: they are etymologically related and suggest wakefulness. Under normal conditions, I can't read attentively between 3:00 and 4:00 in the afternoon, or after 11:00 at night; no amount of sugar, coffee or cold air can boost my alertness. I know this, and yet I persistently try to overcome it, as if effort and will were a match for the body. They're potent, no doubt, but fatigue will win in the end. I sympathize with Simon, and the students in my evening classes. I sympathized with Jason, a fifth grader I taught several years ago. Erratic, exuberant, and exhausting, Jason required as much attention as I could spare. It was my job to follow him and several others to their science class and provide support. Once, when a meeting ran past the bell, I was late to my post. Their class was researching ocean ecosystems, jigsaw-style. I opened the door to find Jason transmogrified, darting from station to station like a clownfish in an aquarium. He raced up to me, his hands fluttering fins under his cheeks, and burbled, "Hi, Mr. Furr. Where were you?" To attend to his work,

Jason needed me to hold him to it. Many a child needs that—a mentor by his side, gauging his tensile strength, helping increase it. Attentiveness and patience are where teaching and learning intersect.

Wait pensively and watch closely. Insight only seems to be spontaneous. There are no epiphanies without a long journey. Legend has it that the Magi crossed deserts to see what they saw. Yeats declared that their eyes are "still fixed" in hopes of finding the "uncontrollable mystery."

It was a Friday morning, the subject was Elizabeth Bishop's early verse. A red fox trotted to the center of the field and struck a pose beneath a work of modern art: a vast metallic V, the arms of which sway and cut shards of light for our eyes to blink at. The fox's pose was Wildean and upstaged the art of the art. I could not continue my eavesdropping on my students' group conversations, because to do so would be to ignore what the fox had to say, which was much. I announced him to my class. We looked and looked. Ted Hughes writes of a fox whose eye—"A widening deepening greenness,/ Brilliantly, concentratedly,/ coming about its own business"—fixes the poet's lonely, unproductive, midnight vigil. A poem follows, or so it goes. To class, I say, "Marianne Moore writes the greatest 20th century animal poems," because I'm not sure what else to say and Moore naturally comes to mind in a Bishop class. As for the fox, he soon left as he came. Had we made an impression?

Early mornings are best, the writers say. The crepuscular space before the daily counting of minutes begins, that is your time for musing and making. It's Monday now, and outside my den window, the dawn chorus sings about business as usual. That sweetness is smoke from my neighbor's first cigar. A car starts. I'm thinking of Anthony Trollope, who had the post office to get to by ten, so he began writing before daybreak. Industrious and disciplined, he kept a tally of his daily page and word count, so that if he "slipped into idleness for a day or two, the record of that idleness" would be there to stare him down. My word count is low, and other duties are calling. I must begin making lunches. How easily daily duties displace concentrated idleness. Twilight on the dewy grass reminds me I'll need to mow. Oh well, the tidiness of mown lawns is generally appreciated in the neighborhood.

My oldest son trots down the stairs with the fox's brightness and begins a project at his desk. Has he dreamed of this, or was it in the seconds between the end of the pee and the last step that the muse descended upon him? Today, while I make the peanut butter sandwiches and frown at the Iraq casualty reports, he draws engines—specifically (as he explains) hydro-powered automobile engines to reduce our carbon footprint. Most mornings, he invents, though occasionally he illustrates, as when he'd read a book about Genghis Khan and drew yurts and Mongol armor. If it weren't for school, he would stay in his pajamas and be inventive all morning. But in the life of every American child, there is school to go to, and there are pages of blanks to be filled in.

You remember filling them in as quickly as possible,

don't you, so that you could get back to Tolkien or your sketchpad or Rubik's cube? My son's worksheets often come home with misspellings and miscalculations. When little attention is required, even less may be given. Look out the window, there's a fox. Estimate the distance from your pencil to his forepaws, from his forepaws to the point of the steel tentacle above him, and from there back to your pencil. A triangle—find its area. Fill it with the fox's thinking.

II

The Unbidden Hymns of Polar Bears

On a hill overlooking the Hudson—a wide, grassy hill that affords the kind of views the 18th century art critic William Gilpin named "picturesque," views that could be adduced as explanations for why the Hudson valley gave rise to a school of landscape painting, for whether clenched tight in fog or, as today, overripe with color, the river, valley, and hills were already art before art found them—on this hill, led along by our dog, who is led by her nose, so our path is serpentine, our pace sporadic, and our destination unclear to me, all of this a mode of proceeding that I generally avoid as one who plans, counts minutes, keeps his shoulder to the wheel, moves inexorably towards ever-receding goals, which is why being compelled to walk the dog on an autumn afternoon may be what's best for me despite my reservations about leaving the desk—

on this hill, following this dog, and finding that despite

the proven value (to productivity as well as soul) of getting up from one's books and going for a walk, neither the view nor the jerking at the leash could wrest me from my anxiety that (notwithstanding the embarrassing absurdity of my having the following made-for-1960's-television aphorism imprinted on my brain) "like sands in the hourglass, so are the Days of Our Lives" (that having been my mother's favorite soap opera,) for I am nearing middle age and have miles to go before I sleep if the aforementioned elusive goals are ever to be met, assuming that diligent labor pays off (cf. the calloused shoulder and heavy wheel)—in short, cresting this hill, dog darting, my mind as cluttered and clotted as the opening sentence in a German philosophical masterwork that a student once borrowed from the library, tried to read in its original and, having come to the end of page two but not the end of the first sentence, impulsively, angrily scrawled "you sadist" in the margins, a message to the author and future befuddled readers—that is to say, on the hillcrest, preoccupied, I was stopped, suddenly, by a goldfinch singing.

Actually, it was his singing in flight—the perfect union of the two—that stopped me: a rising sequence, a falling sequence, aligned perfectly with his dips and dives that scored the painterly Catskill horizon. Eric Miller sees it this way:

Eloquent locket leaping between sweet clouds
swung come hither from the Great Chain of Being

In hindsight, his goldfinch and mine of that afternoon are one. But the truth is that what came to my mind in the moment was Shelley's skylark, the iconic bird who pours "[his] full heart/ In profuse strains of unpremeditated art." Shelley's bird is of course a figure for the poet "singing hymns unbidden."

From the finch, a hymn, from the hills, Frederick Church. Isn't it just like a Romanticist to detect Shelley in birdsong in an autumnal landscape? I had been lifted, thank goodness, from the labyrinth of my worries. But what else might I have seen or heard? How else might I have experienced that goldfinch's song? Often we know what is about to be said because we're at home in this place, among these creatures. It's difficult to notice what's different without being intentional, without seeking out the sights and sounds that bewilder us into new thoughts. Even then we can suffer from myopia and a tin ear.

Samuel and I went to hear John Ashbery read at a celebration of his 80th birthday. At the time, Sammy was eight, bright and earnest, and generally enjoyed "grown-up" events. Nevertheless, the teacher in me was concerned that without a few directions for listening, Sammy might get frustrated. So I told him to listen for words or sentences that he liked, and we would talk about them later. Ashbery read a wide range of poems, including the two-voiced "Litany," joined by Ann Lauterbach. Afterwards, as soon as we were away from the crowd, Sammy volunteered, "I didn't understand much but I liked the line, 'The man with the red hat/ and the polar bear, is he here too?' because you just don't expect to hear that in a poem."

You may be wondering what an eight-year-old expects to hear in a poem. Given that his father's a Romanticist, unbidden hymns and the still, sad music of humanity. Given what passes for poetry in the elementary school curriculum, jingles or (at best and much better) nursery rhymes. Which is why I'm glad Sammy agreed to tag along to Ashbery with me. We both needed to hear something different. True, Sammy had been frustrated, minimally, by what he didn't understand, but not knowing exactly what to make of Ashbery's poetry let him listen to it. On an ordinary day, to hear something unexpected requires willfulness and patience: the will to take up the unfamiliar and the patience to be puzzled.

The images that caught Sammy's attention were from an early Ashbery poem, "Glazunoviana," from his first book, *Some Trees*. For Sammy, instructed to listen for sentences he liked, red hat and polar bear were memorable because they defied his expectations. What stayed with me were the final lines: "In the flickering evening the martins grow denser./Rivers of wings surround us and vast tribulation." For several days, I worried at the worried syntax of the last line, at the unsettling fact that what makes the evening flicker beautifully will also blot it out

But as I reflected on the lines with Sammy, those martins sent me outside the poem and into family history. Papa Harold carved martin houses out of gourds. Once the gourds had dried, he bored a two-inch hole in the belly and extracted its viscera. He painted the shells after cleaning them—he preferred red, though I'm told that martins prefer white—and he suspended them from tall crosstrees in the pasture behind his house. Martins came, though the gourd houses weren't needed. Our pastures were surrounded by forty-foot loblolly pines. This colorful highrise was a variety of unbidden hymn. My grandfather also made countless wooden toys and built porch swings for all of us when we had no porches. His urge to make things yielded a barn full of ungiven gifts.

There were, for example, the tapes. In his youth, Papa Harold had been the church cantor. Leading up to the sermon, he stood before the congregation and lined out hymns, his intonings—enthusiastic or plaintive—intended to stir the passions or trouble the heart. At seventy my grandparents purchased a General Electric cassette recorder and began taping themselves, piano and vocals mostly. Sometimes Papa Harold would punctuate his tenor voice, now gravelly with age, with a few notes on the harmonica. Grandma's arthritis made her prone to accidentals on their tinny piano. In spite of their limitations, with verve they recorded their oeuvre of missionary songs: "I am bound for the promised land," "Brethren we have come to worship," "I'll fly away."

They played the recordings for me once, but they never got around to making copies. I suspect that a search through their musty cabinets or the barn would turn them up. Finding a functional cassette player nowadays would be a greater challenge. But archiving folk art or family voices was not their purpose. The recorder was a listener, indifferent by comparison to a Baptist congregation, but nonetheless attuned to detail. Its breathy whir made them thoughtful in their renderings, made their hearts beat faster when they dared to release some passion. After the performance—for it became that under the circumstances—the tape dutifully stored a version of what they had made. But after the performance, having been heard, they shelved it.

When I played the piano at nights over the summer, I was overheard. Our neighbor and her partner, Tom, passed the warm evenings on their deck. Their cigar smoke, attenuated by the breeze, drifted through our open windows. When I was too tired to read any longer, I would go to the piano and stumble around jazz standards and spirituals, the latter in preparation for my Sunday morning gig at a struggling church in midtown. Calling it a "gig" is too hip and glorious. I've nearly come to accept my limitations as a pianist. I play a few minor things well, I listen carefully to good musicians and imitate them poorly, and I play with heart, even when I'm alone. Early one morning I returned from running, and the neighbors were on the porch to watch the sunrise. Perhaps they had been there all night. Tom raised his hand to wave me over and ask if I was the pianist. I blushed. I hadn't imagined that I played loudly enough to be heard. That's dishonest. I probably *had* imagined that in our small urban neighborhood, windows open to catch the tobacco-laced night breeze, I might be overheard, but thinking too much about it would have frozen my wrists and fingers. I babbled a kind of apology for the noise, to which my neighbor replied that he'd enjoyed listening and that I played like one "who had returned to it with great pleasure."

Rivers of wings surround us and vast tribulation. Should you really be walking the dog at this time of day? Should you be teaching that yet again? Why are you recording yourself, unheard of and slightly off key? Do you really have time for all this porch-sitting and cigar-smoking? But that glimmering, that eloquent locket, those notes you overhear as you swing, or when drag your feet through the leaves on the hill. You've heard that tune before, but it's different this time, isn't it? It is different for your having listened to it, especially now, after so much confusion and so many days of fretting and reflection, in increased age and what comes of suffering, after so much joy.

III
Learning, Aneurysms, and Neil Young

Driving home from class one evening, the radio tuned to NPR's *Fresh Air*, I listened intently to Neil Young talk about aneurysms: how they develop (a thinning and ballooning of the arterial walls,) what they look like ("a twisted bicycle tube"), what happens when they erupt (unpleasant consequences). Neil got his knowledge from experience, for he had recently survived surgery on an aneurysm that was discovered incidentally while he was being checked for an unrelated visual complaint. He described the process in great detail, and though he joked at one point that he had inadvertently turned *Fresh Air* into a medical show, he nonetheless pressed on enthusiastically, speaking with authority, proud of his knowledge, and eager to share it.

The urge to tell is virtually irresistible when we've learned something new, especially when that fascinating new knowledge is something that we had formerly believed to be beyond our ken. Neil had learned about aneurysms because that knowledge directly applied to his life (and near death,) but the enthusiasm and pride of his telling were directly proportional to the apparent complexity of the subject, medicine, and to the fact that all of us could be affected by it.

Life-threatening conditions notwithstanding, you've probably been in Neil's position. Your plane's delayed, you're stuck in the airport. You can't abide the wasted time, so you take out the monograph on the South Sea Bubble even though you know that an airport lobby is not the place for such reading. Nonetheless, you get interested. You find that, while the reading is slow, you're understanding it, that this obscure 18th century English economic fiasco seems strangely relevant to our embattled times. You can hardly contain yourself. Ninety minutes into your flight delay, you whip out the cell phone and after a minute of cursing the state of airline travel, you tell your partner all you know about British imperial economics. A bit bewildered, she listens nonetheless, as I did to Neil, out of love and sympathy, and also because she wonders whether there might be something in this that she could learn (besides that she should say "no" when you ask her if you can tell her about what you've just read.) She is like the wedding guest in Coleridge's "Rime," cornered by the ancient mariner, whose supernatural tale eludes explication but seems important, a combination that holds captive the ill-fated guest:

> I pass, like night, from land to land
> I have strange power of speech;
> The moment that his face I see
> I know the man that must hear me;
> To him my tale I teach.

What the mariner's tale means is a puzzle that you simply cannot avoid trying to solve, as generations of readers, my students among them, could testify. Suspend your disbelief, graciously give the mariner just a few moments to warm up, and you'll find yourself interested, even if in the end you can't say for sure what it all means.

A complex knot will hold your attention. My youngest son loves to tie them, colorful, recondite objets d'art, usually in long webs of kite string anchoring the bathroom door—closed—to the stair rails. Necessity demands that these knots be untied, and an artist is never a handy analyst of his own work. So the job falls to me, father and critic, patient but without the gift of long fingernails. One needs an audience for such work, for explaining how the knot was unknotted proves more difficult than doing the deed. Jacob always asks, and perhaps if I were a mathematician, I could elegantly represent the process in figures and numbers. But I'm a writer, and the best I can do in these instances is shrug and say, "You should've been there."

Was it necessity, rather than the knot's complexity, that held my attention—or for that matter, that collared the wedding guest or held Neil captive in subarachnoid space? I don't think so. Necessity sometimes motivates, but complexity captivates. In school, we too often appeal only to necessity. "You need to know this for the test. You need to pass the test in order to graduate. You need a diploma to get a job." Etcetera. Mother Necessity, however, is not a very engaging speaker. The "what" that she presents, the stuff that needs to be known, has to compel us. It is a truism now in education that subjects have to be made relevant to students' lives. Who can deny this? Any teacher, I dare say, can tell stories of being challenged to make her subject relevant to students, being challenged to get them hooked. But I've learned to beware of talk of relevance. In practice, it equals "what you need to know for the test," the assumption being that the fundamental value of course content is measured by the percentage of questions allocated to it on an exam. Or worse, "relevance" masks an assumption that young people cannot be bothered with the old, the complicated, or the other.

Surely one of the terrible joys of education comes in the moment when we embark on learning something new—terrible, because to do so depends upon our recognizing our limitations, the possibilities of failure, the difficulties that lie ahead, but joyful because the imagination wakes up. In her great poem "In the Waiting Room," Elizabeth Bishop describes an epiphany she had at age seven—actually, three days shy of her seventh birthday, if we credit the poem with historical accuracy. She's waiting while her aunt keeps a dentist's appointment, and while reading a *National Geographic*, she hears her aunt cry out. Though she's not so fond of her aunt, whom she calls " a foolish, timid woman," she suddenly feels as though the cry came from within herself. The sensation fills her with dread and wonder. "You are an *I*," she thinks, "and you are one of *them*." The foreign lands of the *National Geographic* and strange faces in the waiting room all become relevant to her, though she cannot articulate how or why. Doing so, one infers, will be the work of her life in poetry.

As a teacher, I tend to believe there are many Elizabeth Bishops—or mute inglorious Miltons—in our classrooms. Their obstinacy and recalcitrance do not go all the way down to their roots. Presented with a problem by someone who has puzzled over it, knows it well, and wants them to puzzle over it too, they'll see its relevance and get hooked, though not necessarily in that order. Several years ago I tutored in an early intervention reading program called Book Buddies. All of my buddies were in either first or second grade and were struggling with learning to read. Reading—decoding and comprehending—was a complex knot. Little books like *The Cat On The Mat*, let alone *Frog and Toad Together*, presented serious obstacles. But over and over again, I was brought up short by the patience and stamina of these six-year-olds, as they segmented, blended, and slowly, slowly re-read to make sense of "Toad was spinning in the dark." One of my buddies, whom I would later encounter again when I taught sixth grade, made it clear why he persevered. "I want to get to the harder books, you know, one with chapters."

After listening to Neil Young's enthusiastic expose on the brain, I got curious, and late one night online—"late" and "online," a combination conducive neither to sleep nor being alert on the following day—I tried reading a series of medical articles about brain disorders. I will admit to limited comprehension of much of this and will not, subsequently, be performing cranial operations of any kind. However, what struck me and stuck with me was the metaphor lurking in the medical argot. The region around the brain seems to have inspired medieval anatomists to poetry. Beneath the skull is the dura mater, hard mother, whose serous shawl is called the arachnoid for its web-like quality. Between shawl and cerebellum, is the subarachnoid space, filled with fluid, as the medieval heavens were with ether. How did I not know that so much poetry lay outside the brain, far from the heart, and beneath the crust where our hair is rooted? In another life, I may study this, and Neil Young may well be the lead author on the textbook.

IV
Staring Out the Window

What you're saying is important and interesting, the critical distillation of a fifty-minute class discussion that could not, in your estimation, have been more vibrant. You're keeping your remarks succinct; you're gesturing dramatically, moving about the room, crediting students with insights they provided. Almost everyone is either taking notes or watching with what appears to be rapt attention. Almost, you note, because the student in the third desk, second row (the desks are bolted down, you're doing your best) is staring out the window. At the risk of losing focus, you quickly follow—let's call the student "Jane"—you quickly follow Jane's line of vision to the parking lot. Cars, a crow, scraps of a discarded fast-food bag. The crow isn't even eating. Everything is still. When time is up and everyone bolts out the door, you decide that Jane staring out the window is better than Jane fixated on the clock, her reverie being preferable to her counting the seconds until she no longer has to listen to your monologue.

It's possible Jane was listening, just as it's likely that not everyone who scribbled as you talked was writing down what you said. We live in a culture that rewards divided attention. Under desks, cell phones collect and send the latest news. But maybe Jane was in fact focused elsewhere; maybe she noticed something you missed. Gabby, my family's unswervingly optimistic dog, perches on the back of the sofa and stares out the window, her head angled between the shade and the glass. Like a yoga master, she holds this pose for long stretches. What crosses her mind? Is she aware that time is passing? Having established her purpose—to await the return of whichever one of us has left the den—she sits with it, not even aware that she sits with it, though alert to what happens on our block. Her attentive silence is broken only by three things: a squirrel, the mail carrier, and Lucy, a poodle, her arch-enemy from down the street. Gabby's immediate, maniacal barking, an indignant response to the temerity of these intruders, is part of the ritual, though no less sincere for being ritualistic. Every day they come, and every day she barks, her fury real until it suddenly subsides and she reclaims her former, watchful disposition.

"And it came to pass…" What was there in the mean time? Trouble starts in the hallways, as do romances and weekend plans, which suggests that the minutes between the day's major events—the return of the owner, for example, or class, or dinner, or Hockey Night in Canada—are vital, even when they're fleeting. In school we minimize time in transit, that unstructured, if not precisely wasted, time when students are not directly under our supervision. From bell to bell it's a sprint. They may steal a quick kiss, but in theory, there's no time to start a fight, and we thereby gain minutes for instruction—again, in theory. For they'll make their plans on the sly during class, "texting" or "tweeting." When we were they, it was quaintly called "passing notes." Receiving one was an event, though precursory, not the main event. That is ever yet to come, at least when you're a student, preparing the scrapbook of the years before fame and fortune.

From the vantage point of age—teachers being always old—what constitutes transition or the time between, as distinct from the main event, the memorable life of the day, is not so clear as a photo album implies. From snapshot to snapshot, your eye must cross a blank divide of weeks or maybe months, the between-time that did not warrant a photo or that did but you had no camera, the neutral zones of life captured on a flat, earth-tone matte before digital slide shows sped transitions and made them glimmer. Jane stares out the window because, perhaps, your concluding remarks are filler before the event that counts. That stretch of pavement is the matte peopled by her imagination with what comes next. What is worthy of documentation is often past recovery before you realize it. You've turned the pages of a photo album and been surprised by how much you recall of the life between the snapshots. How is it you never photographed the daily chaos of breakfast before school? Not one photo exists of you changing a diaper. How will cultures ten thousand years from now, when babies no longer produce waste or do so into clothing that instantaneously vaporizes it, know how you muddled through?

Whether class or the hallway is the event of note, our weeks are filled with getting from here to there, our days with waiting. Jane Austen's Emma, arguably the busiest of Austen's heroines, has something to teach about life in transition. While her indecisive friend Harriet shops, Emma fills the time:

Emma went to the door for amusement.—Much could not be hoped from the traffic of even the busiest part of Highbury; Mr. Perry walking hastily by, Mr. William Cox letting himself in at the office door, Mr. Cole's carriage horses returning from exercise, or a stray letter-boy on an obstinate mule, were the liveliest objects she could presume to expect; and when her eyes fell only on the butcher with his tray, a tidy old woman traveling homewards from shop with her full basket, two curs quarrelling over a dirty bone, and a string of dawdling children round the baker's little bow window eyeing the gingerbread, she knew she had no reason to complain, and was amused enough; quite enough still to stand at the door. A mind lively and at ease can do with seeing nothing, and can see nothing that does not answer.

For a few semesters, I traveled by bus from the Hudson Valley to New York City to teach a course in Jane Austen and Lord Byron. By contemporary standards, a five-hour round-trip commute, once per week, is no burden; I shared this trip with men and women who make it daily, whereas my time in transit on most days rarely exceeds an hour unless I choose to travel on a bicycle. Whatever the mode of transportation, one wants to make the time productive. On the bus, I searched for ways not to waste the hours and felt intense guilt when, on the return trip, I couldn't concentrate long enough to grade a paper or read a chapter and found myself staring out the window. Along I-87 in New York, there are no bakeries with their smells of gingerbread, and even if there were, the bus ferrying me from Port Authority would cancel the aroma with exhaust. But I did notice that periodically, as if marking the miles, there would be a red-tailed hawk in a treetop. On my last trip, I counted twelve between Newburgh and Kingston, each with his several acres of cleared road bank to survey. I imagine that a hawk's mind is lively and at ease—or at least alive to its narrow but crucial interests—and free from the distractions of diffuseness. But Emma does not watch like a hawk, nor a hawk like Emma. Some matters demand an alertness and focus that prevent ease; seeing nothing is insufficient if the result is hunger. Tranquility gives the mind scope to roam, necessity behooves it to scan, swoop, and cling.

When my sons return from school, where they never stare out windows unless directed to do so by their teachers, Gabby leaps from the back of the couch and greets them with an enthusiasm that would shame the prodigal son's father. Every day she does so. The event never pales. It's like the moment when Cher realizes she loves Josh in *Clueless*, Amy Heckerling's brilliant adaptation of *Emma*. Even if Gabby's enthusiasm does not involve Emma or Cher's degree of self-realization, there are fountains and fireworks nonetheless. I've lost track of how many times I've read *Emma*. A history professor of mine once claimed to have read it forty-two times, and one of my students boasted twenty-four viewings of Heckerling's film. Reading is an event, and if the text has depth and breadth, re-reading offers far more than a review of the story or a re-living of its experiences. You look away from the page and out the window not because you've lost interest but because you need a moment to catch up. Outside a plastic bag clings to the snowbank. A crow watches it curiously. Somewhere nearby there is talking, white noise. Soon the bell will ring.

Leaving a Mark

It was Ronnie struck the first match, sure. But all of us burned down the school library, just like all of us helped rip off the computers.

Here's how it goes: We're tearing along the highway, raising too much hell for worry and common sense to find any room to squeeze in, when Ronnie, who's driving, because he always drives, gets this serious look, yanks the cigar out of his mouth, and says, "Boys, what about all the hair?" No one can really hear him at first because Iron Maiden is jacked up so high. Stephen and Mikey have shotgunned a sixer each by then, and they's playing air guitar with their teeth while the rest of us bitch and groan underneath them because it's crowded in the cab of Ronnie's pick-up.

"Hair, goddamit!" Ronnie shouts and stabs the eject button right when Dave Murray is about to tear loose in "Run to the Hills." You can understand why Ronnie done such a drastic thing, it being the part that kicks the most ass in the whole song. He was about to make a point and had to be heard. But being too drunk to think twice, Mikey jabs the cassette back in, so Ronnie backhands him like he was his red-headed stepchild and yanks the truck off the road. He kills the engine. Mikey's whimpering and sputtering "aw fuck Ronnie, shit Ronnie!" but he's not likely to do nothing else because you're a fool to fuck with Ronnie when he's serious.

"Boys, we got to go back," Ronnie says all sober as funeral homes. "We thought about fingerprints but we didn't think about hairs."

"What the hell are you talking about?" Stephen shouts as if the radio is still on. He's too hammered to take an example from Mikey so he gets Ronnie's hand, too.

Now you got to understand something about Ronnie. One night me and Mikey was watching *The Untouchables* on HBO, it was the first time we'd seen it, we probably seen it thirty times or better now. And you know that scene when Al Capone is walking around the table real quiet and serious and he's carrying a baseball bat, and out of the blue, he just bashes some poor fucker's head to a pulp? Me and Mikey turned to each other after that and said, "Ronnie." It was like a sign. Ronnie ain't big—Capone's scarier looking, for sure. But Ronnie aims to be big time, and he don't fuck around.

"You two is about the most worthless collection of protoplasm," Ronnie sneers. "Just shut up for a minute. I'm saying that we thought to wear gloves, but we didn't cover our heads. And, meaning no disrespect Vern, but you shed like a sheep dog and the rest of us probably dropped a few, too."

I don't feel disrespected. It's true we all got a lot of hair, except Ronnie. I happen to know that Ronnie wishes he could grow a ZZ Topp beard but he's just baby-butt smooth. I say that I don't see his point about leaving hairs.

"DNA test, Vernon," Ronnie says in a Tom Brokaw voice. "They'll comb the library carpet, run tests on ya'll's hairs, and get proof that we heisted them computers. Dumb and Dumber there will just get juvey time but for you and me and Horace, it'll be the State pen."

Horace ain't said much since we scrammed from the library. He'd just sat there chain-smoking Winstons, taking up half the cab and mumbling about Stephen's bony little ass. Stealing computers had been Ronnie's idea, but Horace knew this guy who'd pay us cash for them. And Horace was counting on his share of the take, because he likes to shoot pool, but he sucks at it. "It's a bit late to do anything about that," he says, "If we ain't at Felton by four, Jasper will figure we wussed out and go back home to bed."

"And if we don't do something about all that DNA, we'll be using the money to post bail," Ronnie snaps, as if we'd carpeted the place with our hair. He drives the truck over the median and heads us back north.

Horace squirms and the whole truck lists to the right. He scrunches up his face. "Now Ronnie," he says, and that patented Horace whine is slipping into gear, "I need that cash. Lester says I got five days to pay up. Hell, jail would be safer than me being late again."

"Maybe safer for your fat ass," Stephen screeches, "I'm with Ronnie. How we gonna get all that evidence cleaned up, Ron?"

"Ron." No one calls him Ron. Stephen's sucking up on

account of if he gets clocked again his goddamn tooth will probably come out.

"Can't possibly clean it all up," Ronnie replies. The speedometer is knocking at 100. Horace keeps protesting, which is why I think he ought to get the lighter sentence now, but ain't nobody paying him attention. His whine gets drowned in the whine of the tires on the highway.

"Can't possibly clean it all," says Ronnie again, "So we got to do something more drastic."

Now I reckon that what I say next could hang me, but I got to come clean about this whole matter. It's been troubling my soul, and between that and sharing a cell with Horace, I can't sleep. When Ronnie said "drastic" the first thing that come to my mind was fire. So I said it. "You'd have to burn the place to destroy all that evidence," I says, in just a normal voice as if I was saying "At six o'clock the sun will rise" or "Please pass the ketchup." I weren't suggesting that anything get burned, I swear, but you could say I accidentally lit the spark.

That's all she wrote. Ronnie nods and pats me on the shoulder. Stephen and Mikey starts whooping and hollering, and Ronnie lets them play "The Number of the Beast" eight times straight. Horace is blubbering, and I just feel sick in my stomach. I just keep wishing I was back home in the rack with nothing to look forward to the next day but English for Idiots and Math for Mental Retards. I hate every day of high school and I hate the stock boy job at Winn Dixie that is supposedly a "good place to start for one in my position." But all that dreary shit is better than where I'm headed now at 100 mph. Of course, I won't be able to stop myself from following along, and I'm not going to lie about it: I helped get the blaze going. Hell, I siphoned the gas for it. I can't pull out of something once I'm in, and the fact is that when Ronnie pitched his plan to rip off the new computers, I was charged and ready to go.

Now I felt different when we started torching books. Honest. Not that I care about reading, but setting fire to books felt like sin in a way that stealing computers didn't. It made me nauseous. I mean there was Bibles in there, and *Where the Red Fern Grows*, which I got to admit I did read. Still yet I did my part. Wasn't nothing for it, really, but to do it.

You got to understand something: except for Horace, none of us really cared much about the money we'd make. The money was icing. The cake was pulling off the robbery. So when it looked like we really hadn't pulled it off, and that we was going to get caught, we had to take it to the next level. Otherwise the thrill was gone and the whole game was pointless. At least this way, even if we was caught, we'd done something worth getting caught for. Something that left a mark.

Gavotte II (Approach strong deliveress)

Light Hearts and Wings

A hawthorn wreath hangs over the mailbox on our front porch. Its scarlet berries having faded to pink, it should have been taken down long ago. But while it began as a Christmas wreath, time transformed it into a variety of home accent, and our old house having few such accents (we always intend to do more), we left it up until it became a fixture, like the weathered siding (which needs to be upgraded) or the flag holder (which remains flagless.) Siding, mailboxes, flag holders—the purely functional items of the home—are most in favor when they can be ignored. Either they're doing their jobs, or they're prepared to do their jobs, and we take notice of them only if they fail. The mailbox daily renews our attention, though not the box itself but what it holds, even if the box suffers from a slammed lid when we find bills or rejection slips inside. Décor however has no function beyond pleasing us, so when it becomes invisible on display, its next stop is a yard sale table or the landfill, as soon as anyone takes notice.

The wreath became an exception to the rule. On a December morning, a wren, who had furtively woven a nest into the wreath's inner circle, burst forth at ear level just as I opened our front door to take the dog out. The nest—a pouch of straw and fiberglass fluff from discarded insulation—altered the wreath's purpose and renewed its value, indeed markedly increased it. From that moment, the wreath became at once fully visible and utterly mysterious, functional and sacred. My two sons, my wife, and I immediately reported any sighting of the wren, who is small and stealthy and like the Holy Spirit or Emily Dickinson prefers a low profile despite the vitality of her ministrations. We fretted over the wren's decision to nest here in upstate New York in the winter. On New Year's Eve we purchased a suet feeder and hung it at midnight from fishing line, far enough from the porch railings to make it inaccessible to even the most determined and acrobatic of squirrels.

When I tell this story, people say, "there's a poem in that." True enough. The suddenness of small animals, the way they awaken us from our lethargy, renew the mundane, and initiate reflections upon our creaturely condition, has been a mainstay of poetry. So much so in fact that a new poem about a wren bursting forth would risk disappearing into a cloud of "sudden bird" poems, much as our wreath faded into the dirty grey of the siding. It takes a great poet or at least a great poem to remind us, by example, why the trope became a trope in the first place—to make a lark, and thereby our minds, flicker. One of the skylarks of John Clare, a Romantic era poet of rural England, has neither the fame nor the metaphoric lift of Shelley's better-known bird, but it sprang from the page when I discovered it, belatedly, in a remaindered collection of Clare's verse. In the poem, the lark is disturbed into flight by roving boys at play among the buttercups—"golden caskets," as Clare puts it, because the boys compete to see who can first "pluck the prize":

And from their hurry up the skylark flies
And oer her half formed nest with happy wings
Winnows the air—till in the clouds she sings
Then hangs a dust spot in the sunny skies
And drops and drops till in her nest she lies
Where boys unheeding past—neer dreaming then
That birds which flew so high---would drop agen
To nests upon the ground...

Clare knew birds, and this lark has more of the natural world about it than Shelley's. To be fair, unlike Clare's, Shelley's lyric is no more about the bird than *Hamlet* is about procrastination. But the difference does highlight what makes Clare's lark surprising. Rather than its unbidden hymns, the bird's flight and nest—particularly its nest—are the source of Clare's metaphor and the poem's simple lesson. The boys ridicule the bird, for if they had wings, they claim, they'd build among the clouds, away from all threats. Clare suggests that they're too naïve, perhaps too Romantic, to see the brilliance of the lark's strategy. Inconspicuous among the "dews of morn," the lark's "low nest" is secure though under foot. Both there and in flight, the lark disappears, and this disappearance makes the more often noted song possible. "Then hangs a dust spot in the sunny skies" is masterful in the simplicity of its diction and idea, and in this thirty-line poem it occupies the fifteenth. Having spun away to dust, the lark vanishes at the poem's center, into the clear space between the lines.

Fear launches Clare's lark, just as it did my family's wren. Notwithstanding the chance to inspire poetry, the small creature would clearly prefer to remain unnoticed. Alert, hunkered down, our wren flew because danger seemed imminent, and however unintentionally, we regularly gave her reason to fear when we romped in and out of the front door, always in a hurry. In time, she seemed to determine that flight was unnecessary. Braced and ready, she stayed put, having learned that loud, erratic traffic is normal in her neighborhood, that in fact it signals her beneficial trans-mogrification from novelty to fixture. We grow accustomed to a wren in the wreath. The apparent power differential between our wren and her noisy humans—the legitimate source of her fears—is belied by her sharper reflexes and speed. With wings, she nests contentedly.

Of course our willful ignorance does not apply to all creatures equally. From the perspective of the homeowner, the wren is a squatter whose few inches of turf we happily concede. Others are less welcome to stake a claim. I once stared down a mouse who was stealing into our pantry in the late evenings. I happened to be writing at the kitchen table by dim light when he popped up like a genii from the hairline crack between the baseboard and a cabinet. Imme-diately he sensed that he'd been seen. He sat up on his haunches just at the edge of the lamplight. No longer than my thumb, the color of dust, his countenance dominated by his wide black pupils, he watched me, as if waiting for me to move. I spoke, admitting that he was disarmingly cute but I was tired of holes in the flour sack and frustrated that he'd gnawed himself free from two humane traps. I warned him that a snap trap was in his future. Neither my voice nor anything I said registered a reaction. Rather, he seemed to wait politely for me to finish. Then he flashed into the pantry. The gall of this broke my patience, and in the tradition of cartoon grandmothers, I grabbed a broom from the closet and flung open the pantry door. The mouse had vanished, or, more accurately, slipped through a gap, his escape route, behind the door facing.

It is difficult not to idealize the nest to which the mouse returned, cozy in a corner between the sheetrock and studs, inaccessible to his predators. Like our wren in her secret pouch, the mouse seems to be part of a miniature world parallel to ours, one that remains largely invisible. That world is often the setting of children's stories, where resourceful mice share our creature comforts—matchboxes become beds, misplaced thimbles serve as coffee cups—and sometimes our struggles, so that sewing needles must be transformed into spears. When we're children, the notion that such a world exists nearby must be as much a part of its interest as the cleverness of its trappings. Inside the wall is Crusoe's island, and the mouse has the marooned man's dominion, maybe even a tiny version of his clever umbrella, without his overweening conscience. Interiors are safe, we imagine, and this home within our home is secure, like the cave we create under our blanket. The nest is an emblem of sanctuary and solitude. But, paradoxically, it is so only when no one knows it's there. Discovery is inevitable, and acceptance is in reality only a distant hope. Danger is the fundamental condition of mice and men.

"Your Guinea pigs," explained Cecilia, our family's advisor on pets, "will always dash away when you reach for them because they've been somebody's prey for thousands of years." It's hard to overcome that. The memory of talons is deeply imprinted and quickly recollected. Once the pigs have burrowed in his sweatshirt, they chortle in something akin to gratitude, only to squeal in terror when he gently unearths them to return them to their cage. Burns' "To A Mouse" is the most familiar lyrical meditation on this subject, but I prefer Clare, whose poetic descriptions of nests often become ruminations on risk. His birds vigilantly design tiny bulwarks against invaders. No fortification being impenetrable, Clare maintains that the bulwarks are truly effective only if they release their builder from fear and permit joy, however transitory, the kind of joy emblematized in a skylark's song. The dark side of prudence is paranoia, as Clare implies in one of many of his sonnets in couplets, "The Firetail's Nest." The poem opens with a robin warning that a cat creeps near her young, and it closes with a firetail piping anxiously "the whole day long." But this is not to say that the sonnet begins and ends in fear. Rather, the robin's cry is the first of several birdsongs, each with a different purpose: a "bluecap tootles" as it dines on flies, a chaffinch calls "pink" to a mate, and "in a quiet mood hedgesparrows trie/ An inward stir of shadowed melody." With the exception of the robin's legitimate alarm, joy is the essential motif of the bird-songs, and all the songs, the robin's included, contrast with the firetail's. That bird, whose names—firetail, common redstart, Phoenicurus phoenicurus—conjure brilliance and fires of regeneration, sings the sestet turn in an unexpectedly funereal tone:

> While on the rotten tree the firetail mourns
> As the old hedger to his toil returns
> And chops the grain to stop the gap close bye
> The hole where her blue eggs in safety lie
> Of every thing that stirs she dreameth wrong
> And pipes her 'tweet tut' fears the whole day long

Contrary to his usual practice, Clare provides no details about the firetail's nest. Like the hedger's "gap," it is merely a "hole," and yet the bird's eggs "in safety lie." As the hedger's labors suggest, things fall apart, and mending in the interest of preventing further damage is prudent, not unlike the robin's warning that will stop the cat short of the fledglings. But the firetail's pessimism is unwarranted. The nest may serve its purpose, obscuring the eggs even from a man who works nearby. The "tweet tut fears," as Clare's choice of onomatopoeic adjectives implies, are foolish, borrowing trouble.

I was once a hedger of a different sort from Clare's. For all of spring, I had neglected the border of shrubs between our yard and the neighbor's, and by June the hedge was a ten-foot tangle of poison ivy and maple saplings. I attacked it with a borrowed set of electric shears, the bourgeois broadsword, hacking away at the crown of the hedge and oblivious in my sweat and energy to a robin's nest until, pausing to catch my breath, I spied a blue egg on the ground. From a crack in the shell extruded the partially formed abdomen of a bird. In the nest, which I now saw for the first time, one egg remained. Had the robin been nearby, sounding an alarm, would I have taken care? The grinding shears would have drowned him out. Having been the hedger, how can I not take the firetail's point of view? I am predisposed to tweet-tut fears, taking small comfort in my over-preparedness, anticipating the capriciousness of fate from which no nest is safe. I am most often the firetail.

There is no remedy for feeling insecure in the most secure of spaces or for being a prophet of doom warmed by the sun. But we have our nests, wings and vigilance, and there is virtue in controlled pessimism. Joy coming as a surprise offers an advantage over our being brought up short by suffering and indifference, which are likelier in a world of vulnerable creatures beset by swords and plough-shares alike. In a strange lyric meditation called "The Timber," the English metaphysical poet Henry Vaughan addresses a fallen tree and soberly observes that, "many light Hearts and Wings/ Which now are dead, lodged in thy living bowers." Hearts and wings, those avian parts that signify more than the whole, are life and the potential for flight. Thriving unnoticed, life lodges in life, generations of birds nesting, raising and flying away from the tree until a storm fells it. Before his invocation of mortality—"which now are dead"—Vaughan reminds us of a lightness that is as crucial as it is evanescent. The wings and heart are light, lifting the bird and us, when we notice. We must teach ourselves to attend to the wren as it bursts from the nest. There is no gift-giver, nothing choosing us to be witness to such an event, which makes it all the more luminous and worth holding against the darkness into which every creature soon vanishes.

Hiking back down Peekamoose Mountain in the Catskills, Samuel and I were stopped by a redstart. From a fallen birch, brought down by last winter's late heavy snows, it flitted to a hemlock and penny-whistled. It fanned its wings and tail, hopped to a stone, and flew back to the birch. All along it chattered and nodded, curious and agitated. It made this round—actually a triangle—repeatedly while we watched and light decanted from the canopy. As if something were about to happen, as if awaiting the outcome of an incantation, we were fixed to the border. But this was it. The performance was the fulfillment. Being present folds us into what ends when the warbler flies away. We sit on a fallen timber to make something further of it, this startling aside, this mere decoration, becoming a place to dwell, functional and sacred.

War Wounds

Dennis Pinkerson, the oldest kid on our street, had a four-inch, purple scar along his hairline. It was thick and ridged like a worm, and he claimed it was where the Comanche Indians had scalped him. Never mind that we lived on a cul-de-sac in Salem, New Jersey, in the middle of the twentieth century. My sister and I were preschoolers and believed Dennis unquestioningly. After all, he was in fifth grade and had been out west in his family's camper when his dad came back early from the war in Germany.

In time, we would begin to doubt that Dennis' scar had come from a tomahawk, though his cold stare always stopped us short of questioning it. But by then we had scars of our own to show off. Milly, my sister, had a divot beside her left eye, dug by an infected pock during her bout with chicken pox. I sported a thin, pink eraser line just below the Fruit of the Loom elastic where my appendix had been removed. My best friend, Theodore Adams, had a lightning bolt on top of his left foot. A bowl of table scraps had shattered there when he dropped it on the way to feed their German Shepherd. Rachel Stein from three houses down had no visible scars. But because she'd broken her arm three times, everyone agreed that the bones must be gnarled and knotted with scar tissue.

More impressive than all of these, however, were the scars of our fathers: the missing leg and blast-blinded eye of Mr. Pinkerson, the bits of shrapnel dug in like clams under Mr. Stein's skin. War wounds—we children had nothing on those. It was the defining truth of our childhood that none of us had suffered, or would suffer, as our fathers had.

Only Marty Schmidt came close, because his dad was killed in action right before the war ended in Europe. I was four, and I never remember seeing Mr. Schmidt, except in his closed, flag-draped casket. The flag impressed me, and how the sombre veterans handled it: marched over to it, lifted it off the coffin with an air of reverence, snapped and creased it, folded it with mechanical precision into a tidy parcel, and all but knelt with it before Marty and his mom. Naively, I envied them. I felt a twinge each time I rode my bicycle past their house, where the flag waved just as the national anthem promised it would.

My envy deepened after my father returned from the war. Not that I wanted to have lost him. It was just that the Schmidts' loss was a badge of honor. No one questioned their right to grieve. The scars of Mr. Pinkerson and Mr. Stein were similar : what clearer evidence of valor was needed? My father's wounds, on the other hand, proved to be obscure and internal, manifesting themselves in peculiar behaviors that called upon tolerance and pity rather than admiration or sympathy.

For example, after the war my father stopped sleeping.

Days would go by and none of us would see evidence that he'd lain down, or even paused in his manic productivity. His eyes sunken and gray, his movements slow and clumsy from exhaustion, he'd nevertheless pour a cup of coffee and start a new project: open up the next book in his stack, re-grout the bathtub, strip and refinish the hardwoods, revise a lecture that he may never be invited to give. He claimed that he couldn't afford to waste time in bed. He had too much ground to make up in his doctoral studies because of the years lost to the war, and the home improvements could not be put off any longer. My mother went along with this. "He's just happiest when he's working," she'd say.

But all of us eventually understood his real reason for avoiding sleep. He was afraid of the things he saw when his eyes fell shut. On the rare occasion that he dozed off in our presence, he would startle awake, shouting and taking cover. Once, bursting up from his desk in the living room where we all read quietly after dinner, he hurled a glass paper weight into the soundboard of our baby grand piano. There was a sudden sound of glass splintering and strings snapping, like an orchestral rendering of an explosion. Milly began crying hysterically, and mama just sat there, stunned. Agitated, my father skittered over to the piano and began plucking shards out of the strings. He grew increasingly shaky and flustered, and not knowing what else to do, I went over to help. Before I could reach for the first sliver, however, his hands flashed to my wrists, gripping them so hard that I squealed. He let go abruptly, apologized, threw up his hands, and headed for the coffee pot. My mother vacuumed the soundboard and phoned a tuner the next day. We never talked about it.

Silence was my family's prescription for dealing with my father's odd behavior. As for my father, his self-prescribed therapy for nightmares was caffeine. Everywhere he went, in fact, he carried a thermos of coffee in an olive drab knapsack, the way people nowadays carry epipens or albuterol inhalers. His teeth were the color of old Hushpuppies, his sweat smelled like a diner. Many times, after midnight, I have been startled awake by the kettle whistling. For my father, it was never too late in the evening or early in the morning for Maxwell House.

I recall one of the times in particular that his midnight perambulations woke my sister and me up. Milly had lost her first baby tooth and wanted nothing to do with the tooth fairy. Our mother had assured her that the fairy only came if you wanted her to, but Milly wasn't convinced. She tossed and turned in the bunk below me, certain that the fairy would come in the night and demand the tooth. It seems we'd only just fallen asleep, after hours of this, when the kettle screeched. Milly woke up. No matter that she'd been awakened by my father before—tonight she insisted that the tooth fairy was in the house. Exasperated, I crawled down the ladder and took her by the hand, "Come on," I said, "I'll show you it's just daddy."

We crept down the stairs, Milly simpering but clinging tightly. My father was, as I suspected, in his den. He was often there, translating Hölderlin's marginalia, or poring over the letters of some obscure thinker who had known the

German poet. A steaming cup waited within quick reach. That night, he stood in the yellow glow of his desk lamp, his back to the door. He was gesticulating with his pencil, as if he were conducting a symphony, and he was reciting something in German. He became increasingly animated, his muttering undergoing a rapid crescendo, until suddenly he slapped the desk in fury and slapped himself across the cheek. Milly and I both squeaked. He didn't notice. He started over, quietly, baton in the air, and never knew that we were watching him. It terrified us, and we sought mama's bed. There was always plenty of space for us to crawl into bed beside her, and we were never turned away.

No doubt, my father's lack of sleep and abuse of caffeine aggravated his many nervous tics, the most pronounced of which was a flinch. At regular intervals, he would jerk his right hand upwards (he wrote and drank with his left, fortunately.) Sometimes, the flinch was slight, his hand never making it above his waist. At others, it was as if he were shielding his eyes from a blast. This tic—along with a tendency to wince without provocation and blink too often—grew worse over my childhood. By the time I was about to enter high school, and the war was far enough behind that we kids dared joke about it, the flinch and the insomnia had earned my father the nickname "Shell-Shocked" among my classmates.

I first heard it in the summer before my freshman year. I was in the locker room at the community pool; Marty Schmidt and some new kid he'd befriended were in the showers. "That twitching guy?" Marty said, apparently in response to a question from the new kid. The showers began to spray. He raised his voice. "That's 'Shell-Shocked.' Got messed up—in the head, you know—during the war. His son's in our class—he's not messed up, but I think he's probably pretty sensitive about his pop. Who wouldn't be?" The showers cut off, the two of them stepped into the locker room, dripping, and suddenly we were all staring at each other. I just shrugged and went along with it. I introduced myself as Shell-Shocked's son. When you're thirteen, you laugh at your parents' flaws to prevent being crippled by embarrassment. Sympathy for them is still decades away.

It didn't help that my father, whose interests and aptitudes were largely unemployable in our community, was a history teacher at McKinley High School, which in our small town meant that every child spent two years under his tutelage, becoming well-acquainted with his strangeness. A devoted scholar of Romantic period literature—German romanticism, in particular—my father was given six sections of U.S. history by McKinley's principal, Rupert Howell, who "looked out for veterans." I suppose Mr. Howell figured that my father knew enough about the subject to teach it to the average seat-warmer at McKinley and that what he didn't know, he'd learn.

I dreaded being at the same school as my father, let alone in his class. I avoided eye contact with him, and I never let myself be seen walking or talking to him. As it turned out, most of the time he just seemed eccentric, a socially-acceptable trait in a high school teacher at the time. Regardless of the season, he wore a brown corduroy sports coat and a turtleneck shirt. He paced when he lectured, never looking at the class, always taking the same number of steps—seven—before changing directions. Then there was the coffee cup, appended to his left hand like a prosthetic device. It was odd, but only marginally more so than the cigarettes that were crutches to most of our other teachers.

The flinch, however, was his trademark, and I must have blushed at him daily in history class. In the middle of a lecture, his free hand would fly up out of the blue with force enough to deck a sailor, and kids would gasp, expecting a hot brown shower. And yet his left hand allowed only the slightest ripple on the surface of the coffee. Never a drop spilled. It was a show that kept students entertained through tedious lectures on Federalists and Anti-Federalists, the Grant administration scandals, or monetary policy's vexed history. My father was nothing if not a devoted scholar, and having been given this U.S. history project, he set out to learn all there was to know so that he could be a more informed teacher. But his detailed, carefully-prepared monologues were more suited to graduate students than a classroom of future mechanics and cosmetologists. Only the two or three smart kids paid attention. The rest watched the coffee cup show, and I sketched in my notebook.

By Christmas break, the coffee cup show had begun to lose its impact, and attempts were made to get my father to recount war experiences. I should have told everyone that it was a lost cause. For how were they to know that he was any different from Mr. Kaminski in life science, who could be easily diverted from lipids and proteins to life as a P.O.W. in the South Pacific. He spun harrowing yarns of buddies in solitary confinement forced to eat their own "fecal matter," as he called it, and of comrades beaten to death for refusing to take orders from a Japanese officer. Kaminski was better than *Bridge on the River Kwai* and kept every one of us, flunky and square alike, riveted. Not so my father. Surely he had tales to rival Kaminski's; after all, he'd been across France and Germany in the last years of the war. But he refused to talk about it, even to his family, and would merely shake his head silently when a student tried to wheedle a story out of him.

During my first year as his student, I became increasingly embarrassed by his quirks and tics, to the point of resentment. The least he could do, I felt, was tell a little about his experiences in the war, if for no other reason than to bring honor to our home to balance the weirdness. I began to be troubled by doubts. What if he never told stories, I wondered, because he had none to tell? I'm certain that I wasn't alone in thinking this. Once, after a particularly difficult midterm exam—my father's tests were notoriously hard—Willy Schumaker speculated, openly and shamelessly despite my presence, that Shell-Shocked had spent the war in a looney bin. We all knew that Wally had just failed the first semester of my father's class—he couldn't possibly have passed that exam—and that the remark was sour grapes. Everyone "pshawed," told him to put a sock in it, declared that he was just sore about flunking—in short, made all sorts of reprimands on my behalf. But secretly they were fascinated by the idea, even convinced of it. I'm sure they were, because I was.

It got to the point that I could think of nothing else. Everything about my father began to grate on me: his reticence, his twitches, his thermos. I wanted evidence that all of his bizarre traits—his reticence, his twitches, his thermos—were somehow justified, that he'd experienced something worth causing me such embarrassment. Surely he owed me that much, I thought, and because he wouldn't talk about the war, I felt justified in researching his involvement on my own. The natural place to start was among his things in his den.

I faked illness on a Thursday, when my mother always went grocery shopping and stopped at the public library. I estimated that she would be gone for two hours, giving me plenty of time to poke around my father's closet and desk. Besides, I was convinced that if she caught me, she'd turn a blind eye. Wasn't she as curious about this as I was? I would be liberating her, I reasoned, from the tyranny of his secrecy.

When she was ten minutes out of the house, I began my search. I imagined there'd be a box of soldier's paraphernalia among his things—surely even he had kept it. I went for the closet first. His wardrobe held no surprises. There were two brown corduroy jackets with matching pants, five turtlenecks—three black, two cream—and a pair of loafers. It was just as everyone joked at school: the man was as bland as his lectures. I shivered.

Under the loafers was the box I'd imagined finding, wrapped tightly in tan paper and sealed with packing tape. How was I supposed to open it without being found out? I didn't allow myself to think much about this dilemma before fetching a kitchen knife and opening the seams. I hadn't come this far to be stopped by tape.

Inside was a musty, woolen uniform, drab green and lifeless, staring up at me like a disinterred corpse. A menagerie of metals was clustered in one corner, and corporal's stripes were sewn onto the sleeve. There was nothing else: no photograph of platoon buddies, no relics of the battlefield, no cherished letters from home.

I was discouraged, but there was still the desk to search. It was cluttered with notecards, books, and papers, but there was a method to the clutter. There was a miniature cityscape of notecards, stacked at various heights like buildings, each with a label: Hölderlin marginalia, Hölderlin and English romantics, Hölderlin French reception, and so forth. The papers were likewise organized in stacks, though most were letters from libraries responding to my father's queries about their holdings. Everything on that desk was about his scholarly interest—nothing about his history lectures. He kept all of that on his desk at school, I figured. More importantly, there was nothing there that touched on his past. It was all about Hölderlin. Even his journal, a thick leather-bound notebook that he wrote in every night after supper, was taken up entirely with reflections on lines from Hölderlin.

Why was he so impassioned by that man's work? As I

rifled through notes and papers, finding nothing of interest to my pursuit, my resentment of my father burned hotter than ever. I grew careless, even reckless, allowing papers to crumple under my fingers and spill onto the floor. The desk slowly became a shambles.

I had only one place left to look—a shelf of library books that leaned precariously against his desk. He had built the shelf one afternoon after my mother, in a rare moment of gumption, complained about the towers of books on the floor. The shelf was impeccably constructed—it was, after all, my father's handiwork. Nevertheless, it bowed under the burden of Sturm und Drang, its shelves overburdened and braces cracked. Figuring that I would come up empty-handed, I had already decided not to risk pulling a volume off and causing the shelf to collapse. But there was one book, navy blue and frayed, that jutted out slightly from the others on its row: a translation of Hölderlin's verse. I pulled it out to thumb through it.

The text was elaborately illuminated, the margins filled with intricate art and script. Had my father drawn this? What at first appeared to be the serpentine twists of rose vines, however, proved upon closer inspection to be barbed wire. I brought it under his desk lamp and discovered that the wire was constructed of fine print, in my father's hand, precise and legible. It was a necrology of the war dead, named soldiers and unnamed civilians, with brief notes on the circumstances or places of their deaths. Periodically, the network of wire would break to give way to a platitude or a gruesome sketch from battle. Scattered among the wires of "Brot und Wein," for instance, were gaping faces, death-masks with twisted jaws and fragmented skulls.

In the white space after that long poem, the graphics culminated in an account dated Easter, 1944: "Unknown girl, age 8 or 9. From a rooftop in Leipzig, I watched the crawler tracks of a tank snatch up a girl who was fleeing her apartment, drag her underneath and chew her up, and shit her out in bloody chunks. The second and third tanks ground her remains into the dirt. *Satt gehn heim von Freuden des Tags zu ruhen die Menschen...*"

I scribbled the lines on a blank notecard and replaced the book. My heart was pounding. I felt as if I had stolen something. But the book had been hung out there like the forbidden fruit, I rationalized. I told myself that my father had probably wanted it noticed, even as I scurried about, carefully smoothing and replacing all of my father's papers. I must have been afraid of being found out, and surely my father did suspect me, though he never confronted me or even mentioned that his desk had been tampered with. Fear of being caught, however, is not the feeling I remember. What I recall is the overwhelming desire to make things as they were before—to be angry and embarrassed again, to be ignorant of what tormented my father, just as he wanted us to be. And I recall the heaviness of realizing that that was quite impossible.

By the weekend, sun and the idea of approaching spring had brought everyone in our neighborhood into their yards with flats of impatiens, clippers, and hoes. My father emerged grudgingly. Being outdoors impelled social contact, which my father always preferred to avoid. However, some lawn work was incumbent upon him to appease the neighborhood association. Snows had taken down several tree limbs around our house—the yard was a disaster—so he was creating a brush pile at the back of our property. Milly and I helped, and while landscaping was not my father's forte, he was as efficient and thorough in this job as in all things. By early afternoon, there was not the smallest twig left on our lot.

We were resting by our mound of brush, my father pouring coffee from his thermos, Milly and I panting and sore, when Dennis Pinkerson and his father wandered over. Having graduated high school, Dennis lived nearby and worked for his father's plumbing company. He was a loner—we rarely saw him. Today, he had been pruning trees under his father's direction. Like the platoon commander he'd once been, Mr. Pinkerson barked orders at Dennis, heavily accented with venom and curses. His false leg made him lurch when he walked. As he shook my father's hand, his glass eye stared away from us, as if he were keeping watch on the skies.

Mr. Pinkerson was as pleasant and neighborly with us as he had been vitriolic with Dennis moments before. "Den and me were wondering if we could chuck a few limbs onto your pile," he said. "We figured if it stayed nice, why, the lot of us might consider making a bonfire and roasting a wiener or two."

My father flinched. He'd find some way to avoid the bonfire, although he didn't mind sharing the pile.

"Our pile's your pile," he laughed awkwardly and took a long swig of tepid coffee. Mr. Pinkerson nodded, and he and Dennis went back to gather limbs. I went along to help. Dennis shouldered the two longest branches and hoisted them up. As he balanced them, I caught his eyes for the first time that day. They were empty and cold, like the night sky, and the purple scar on his forehead seemed to fester and throb. I looked over at Mr. Pinkerson, who stood holding a stick under his arm like a rider's cane. I felt the heaviness again, as if the weight of all the pain and sorrow from the war suddenly rested on my shoulders. And at that moment, I would have given my own right eye and leg to believe that Dennis Pinkerson had been scalped by Comanche Indians and lived to tell the tale.

Afterlife

A thrush passed a few weeks of his introverted life in our back yard in Virginia in 2002. Over breakfast, classical radio, and the high-decibel chatter of my children, I heard the bird's song, liquid, reverberant, and melancholy, issuing from the fen behind our house. I had been re-reading Whitman's great elegy, "When Lilacs in the Dooryard Bloom'd," and on a poetically-inspired hunch, I flipped to the thrush in my Peterson's. Then, behold, the bird kindly presented himself on the railing of our deck. He sang while in plain sight, as if he knew the birding tyro he was dealing with. He was a wood thrush, and Whitman's is a hermit, but the technicalities in this instance made no difference. His song was elegiac, and elegy was to be the mode of my family's summer.

One of my wife's closest friends, Erica, died later that month. She was a young mother, capable, bright, gracious to a fault. She was healthy and out for her routine run when she went into cardiac arrest. A child saw her fall and sought help, but the minutes without oxygen left her unable to recover. For a week, she lay in a coma—a netherworld, in which her friends and family wavered between hope and despair, between chatting with her about the day and accepting that only her unresponsive body remained alive. Her mind, her self, was no longer there. Soon her body, too, gave way. She died, peacefully and too soon.

Under the circumstances, death is often considered a mercy, and who, in imagining her own death, doesn't wish for a peaceful departure? But the death of a young parent, like the death of a child, is cataclysmic. A void opens, and all light bends into it, leaving those who grieve in darkness and putting the order of things permanently askew. Among a parent's greatest fears is that her young family will be broken by death—that her children will never really know her or recall her smell, her feel, her love for them. My wife and Erica had discussed these fears on sunny days at the playground, when the sun itself and the bliss of their children made mortality remote enough to discuss with candor, even self-effacing humor. How silly, after all, how egotistical, to imagine what a loss your own demise would be! Yet at Erica's death, we mourned deeply for the experiences that she and her children would not share.

On the morning after she died, I rose before sunrise to run the hills near our house. Erica haunted that run, as her memory has haunted many of my morning runs since then. Taking across the long hill by the city high school, I recalled a chance meeting with her on a run five years earlier. On a Saturday morning during my first year as a public school teacher—that storied year from which no teacher emerges unscathed—I was out running hills to clear my mind when she jogged up, pushing a stroller. A model elementary school teacher, Erica had been an instructor in a class that I took to get my teaching license; she had been pregnant at the same time as my wife, and we had planned to get our new families together. Recognizing me, she stopped, smiled broadly, and put a hand on her hip. Erica *always* stopped, and she had the broadest smile.

"Derek! How's Caroline and that little Sammy."

"No one's sleeping a lot," I said, bending over to peek at Max, then only a few weeks old, "but everybody's basically content."

"Well, sleep, who needs it really," she replied, gesturing towards Max, whose blue eyes were wide open. "How are things at Walker School?"

I grimaced. I told her that I had been brooding on my fitness for teaching urban, public school kids and had concluded that, while it had been a noble idea, I really belonged in a university English department, among introverted faculty who could do little damage to their pupils, even with poor teaching, and who usually manage to inspire a choice few to read poetry that might otherwise fade away. I should go back to that, I allowed, or at least to a small rural school, like the ones I had attended and idealized. I just couldn't connect with the urban kids, I confessed, and worried that I was a waste of their time.

Erica nodded, sympathetically. "I've been there. Tidiout, Pennsylvania, where I grew up, sounds like where you grew up: tiny, homogeneous. And the little Christian college where I did my undergraduate work wasn't much different. Then I came down here to teach. That was an eye opener. It's hard. But you'll be okay. You have something to give these kids, and they need you. I found that out. You'll be fine—give it time. Now, what is Caroline's email address? We keep meaning to get together!"

To be reassuring, truly reassuring, is a gift. It requires equal parts sympathy and insight. You must be generous with time, genuinely interested in the downcast, slow to judgement but confident enough to speak plainly. Being so interested in others, interested enough to offer true reassurance, was one of Erica's defining qualities, and I benefited from it. Five years after I ran into her on that spring morning, I'm still teaching those urban kids. And if I could run into Erica now, we'd talk about those kids with shared wisdom and weariness, humor and affection.

In the circuit of hills around Charlottesville High, there is a steep decline by the city's yard-refuse field—less a field than a giant bowl, fecund with decaying oak leaves and pine boughs, generating black soil so rich that it reeks. In June, the field fills with vetch and thistle, morning glory and sweet pea, all quivering with sparrows. The steam of rotting things had just begun to rise when I ran past the chain-link fence that borders the field. An indigo bunting perched on the nearest link, and each time I came close to him, he darted just a few feet further down, watching me. I don't know why I fixed on that bunting, but I made a point of going that same route the next day and the next, and every morning the bunting appeared until the morning after Erica was buried.

Now, I am a skeptic, but with a carefully-repressed yen for the metaphysical—I *want* to believe in the soul, and in an eternity that is not limited merely to human legacies. Doing so is difficult. On the night of Erica's memorial service, the hospital chaplain—a young, articulate woman who had been pastor to the Fulmers and Druggans while Erica lay dying—invited all of us to "share stories of Erica." There was no homily or hymn, no prayer committing Erica to the bosom of God or the shining ranks of the saints. As we constructed it that night, by candlelight, in the tiny gothic chapel on the fringes of Mr. Jefferson's university, Erica's afterlife was stories, recollected and retold. From the interplay of narratives, specific themes inevitably emerge, and Erica's selfless grace was palpable—truly present among us—as friends and family came forward with stories to tell. Stories of her passion for teaching needy children, of her joy in motherhood and her sense of humor towards its demands; stories, like the one that I could not muster the courage to tell, of her willingness to put aside her plans to give time to a friend.

I've rarely been to a more affecting memorial service, and I've been to many. "Carry her grace with you," the minister commissioned us in closing the service, "as you continue to recall and tell her story." It's a heavy benediction: carrying the good news of Erica's life is up to those of us who are left. Her afterlife is up to us. The word is before and remains after the flesh—on this, Christian and post-structuralist and existentialist can likely agree. But stories change, and words get lost in the din of modern life (even now, window open, I lose my words in the screeching of leaf blowers, banshees of autumn.) The soul, I want to believe, is beyond words, a thing we rarely see manifested, articulated, except as it is flying away.

Later that summer, I traveled to North Carolina to visit the mother of my closest friend, Keith. His mother, Eunice, was dying of cancer. This would be our last visit. We all knew that—Eunice, her husband Bill, Keith, and I. Imminent death is palpable, thick as a clouded night, but we couldn't speak of it, or of the fact that I'd come to say goodbye. At what moment do you actually say the word, its blessing having long been overwhelmed by the sense of finitude? To do so takes resolve, courage, and love, and I had only the third of these.

"Good to see you," Bill called from the hallway as I entered their small house. His eyes began to tear, but he recovered himself with a typical witticism. "We're in chambers at the moment…" he said, gesturing with a washcloth towards the parlor. Then he shuffled off, gathering up gauze and poultices as he went, to complete the ablutions of his patient.

The door slightly ajar, I could see Eunice in her wheelchair, her tortured and tiring body awaiting her husband's ministrations. Her back was to the door, and her head rested on her hand. She was weary. I thought of how often her cancer had gone away and returned—cancer always seems to return, like the unwanted guest in fairy tales who keeps coming back and expects more each time. Over the past six years, the cancer had come back so often that Eunice's body had little left to offer.

While Bill did his work, I waited in the kitchen with Keith. An old clock radio, the large wooden kind with silver dials and Roman numerals, rattled the jaunty final movement of Beethoven's Seventh. It was ironic, for Keith's kitchen was where I'd first heard a Beethoven symphony, nearly twenty-five years before. I had spent countless hours around the Smiths' kitchen table in my adolescence, getting incidental lessons in high culture and debate, even a few in the social graces. Transplanted from Boston to provincial Union County, North Carolina, Keith's family was practically foreign. Many things set them apart: classical music and public radio, an irrepressible New England liberalism and Bostonian pronunciation of "car," his parents' college education, Catholicism, and Irish roots. They ate exotic foods like baked Ziti and Indian pudding, and they waited until Eunice sat down before digging in. In a community of Baptist teetotalers, Bill confessed a love of beer, and Eunice occasionally had wine with dinner. It was in knowing them, and falling in love with their difference, that I discovered my own deeply-repressed desire to venture out.

Though in his eloquence and love of story, Bill usually drove the conversation on those evenings, it was Eunice who presided over their small family. In this, at least, we were similar. For the Smith family, like my own, was a matriarchy. Granted, my mother was sentimental, and Eunice was a realist, but both wielded power through their indefatigable attention to the practical life of the family and their singular knowledge of what made it tick. They were economists, in the fullest sense of the word. "You've done well," Eunice was to compliment Keith later that day, referring to his efforts to manage his parents' finances now that she no longer could. "You've made it easy for me," he would reply, holding her carefully tabulated ledgers.

Disease delights in disorder. The chambers of the terminally ill become littered with emesis basins, coils of tube, sterile syringes…reminders of the disarray inside the patient's body. But Eunice's sickroom was as orderly as her bookkeeping. Bill invited us into the parlor, a tiny, well-appointed room tastefully furnished and home to Eunice's modest collection of Hummel figurines. I was struck by how carefully Bill had arranged the paraphernalia of cancer treatment in tidy piles under tables, in corners, behind chairs. Eunice, too, had been arranged carefully on the sofa with pillows to support her. A quilt obscured her distended belly and withered legs. Towels had been draped over her colostomy bag. Altogether the parlor gave Eunice a slight edge over the multiple humiliations of dying.

She was busy when we came in. Through heavy lids, she was double-checking Bill's grocery list. The mundane demands of quotidian living persist, I thought, even for the dying. Bread must be bought, grass mowed, bills paid. The phone, incessantly ringing, must be answered. A romantic, I will no doubt, in my hour of death, rage against these distractions from the mortal drama at hand. But it was soon clear that Eunice took comfort in them. She handed Bill the list and nodded approval. Throughout the morning, she kept tabs on the goings-on around the house—the paper's arrival, the mail's arrival, Bill's bustling in the kitchen. Despite her immobility, she attended to the particulars of hosting, offering me drinks and snacks. My own conversation—weak, alas, even under the best circumstances—amounted to detailed reports on my children: swimming lessons, tent camping, Little Red Readers, scrapes, bruises and bumps. Throughout the morning, I babbled. Eunice smiled sadly, but if I paused, she gestured for more. It seemed to be what she wanted to hear. Those things, after all, are life, and life was what she was being forced to leave.

Eunice was able to say little. Speaking the simplest phrases rendered her breathless and more susceptible to the pain that she silently resisted. Thus far she had refused methadone, preferring panged alertness to numbed oblivion. Her stoicism was remarkable, if ill-advised, and her nurses and family had encouraged her to compromise. Their success had been modest. She had come around to accepting small doses of a nausea medication, lorazepam. Late in the morning, as I rambled on about Sammy's reading, she gestured towards the door and whispered, "The black bottle." Keith left to convey the message to his father. Eunice gazed at me apologetically, as if ashamed to admit that she was suffering. Then, to my surprise, she smiled and blushed. "That medicine for nausea," she explained, "You see birds." It was an admission of guilty pleasure, like confessing a weakness for chocolate. For a moment, the darkness of the room dispersed, as if we had been under a canopy of starlings who, either bored or nervous, suddenly abandoned their posts. "You deserve birds," I replied, and as Bill squirted a tiny vial of the potion in her mouth, I imagined her sailing to Byzantium, greeted by birds of hammered gold.

The remains of that day organize around an imagery of birds. While we ran errands to give Eunice a break, Bill talked poetry. He recited Gerard Manley Hopkins' "The Windhover" on the sidewalk in front of Harris-Teeter Supermarket after we'd bought groceries. He leaned on his cart. I shifted a case of bottled water from hand to hand.

"In your studies in English literature," he began, "did you ever memorize poetry?"

My memory is a sieve, and despite my best intentions, doesn't retain even my favorite lines. This is a sore spot for me, a fact that Bill couldn't have known or he might have saved himself from my apologetic blather. I admitted that I had never in my woefully numerous years of schooling been asked to memorize a poem, a fact which I counted a shame because I now found memorizing impossible and yet, as a reading teacher, was often in a position where reciting verse would be invaluable, not to mention impressive. I recalled that my dissertation director had been able to spin out yards of verse—high verse, low verse, impenetrable verse, whole stanzas of Wordsworth, "The Trees," even Gertrude Stein. It was a skill that he claimed he owed to his mother, who read and recited poetry to him from the moment of his birth. I tentatively planned to require my students to get poetry by heart, I announced, except that it seemed unethical to ask them to do something that I couldn't, considering that my memorization muscle had atrophied beyond recovery.

Bill nodded through all of this, too polite to cut me off. "I still carry in my memory many of the poems from my school days," he said, when I'd finally finished, "but 'The Windhover' is my favorite. If I'd had the wisdom of age when I was writing my thesis, I'd have focused on Hopkins instead of Keats. I love Keats, don't misunderstand me, but I find that Hopkins speaks to much of my experience of life and faith…" He cleared his throat and struck an orator's pose, "'No wonder of it: sheer plod makes plough down sillion/ Shine, and blue-bleak embers, ah my dear,/ Fall, gall themselves, and gash gold-vermillion.'"

He smiled, proud as a school boy, and returned his rattling cart to its dock. Those were lines that he had meditated upon so often in his nearly 70 years of life that their oblique diction had become a source of spiritual clarity. He saw no need for commentary or explication.

It wasn't the first time I'd heard Bill declaim a portion of "The Windhover," but never in the past had he recited only the final tercet. Those lines lay claim to light in spite of darkness. Rust, ash, mortified flesh—the bleakness of the fallen world is mere obfuscation, they maintain. Facing his wife's imminent death, Bill clung like the poet to the promise of second birth. Within Eunice's wasted body, a soul awaited release.

Eunice died a week later, peacefully, before the storms and heat of August descended. I returned to Whitman in the days after her death, to his solitary and persistent thrush, whose song, filtered through the poet, is kaddish for the thousands of young lives destroyed by the Civil War. Near the end of the elegy, Whitman asserts that the bird's song is "tallied" by the voice of his spirit—that it is accounted for, recorded, and interpreted by his troubled soul. In essence, he puts the song to words. The thrush calls death a "mother," imagining her as creator rather than destroyer, as the gentle "deliveress" who comes on "soft feet." Her purpose is to deliver us from suffering, for life is suffering. Reflecting on the thrush's song, as well as the lilac and distant star which have factored heavily in the imagery of his elegy, Whitman claims that the very act of mourning has released his soul to sing, and in that singing he has become one with the "lilac and star and bird"—rejuvenation, eternity, and poetry. Without death there is no poetry; without poetry, there is no life.

Besides coincidence and an abiding sadness, a very real experience of the eternal binds Erica and Eunice's deaths together for me. I am surprised by my own security that they continue to live, just in a way that we are poorly equipped to imagine. For in spite of my affinity for the sobering landscapes of existential thought, and despite the fact that I'm far better at explaining why heaven cannot exist than at describing what I think it looks like, I believe that I caught glimpses of the afterlife last summer. Eunice and Erica are there. They're part of what poets try to represent, and what songbirds sing.

Gigue
Ending with Joy and Insects

> "…and then it was/There interposed a Fly"
> —Emily Dickinson

On stage were twelve horn players, led by a Hungarian trombonist in a concert of contemporary composed music for brass. Trumpet, trombone, tuba, cornet, Sousaphone, flugel and French horns, each was attached by a tight-lipped kiss, so firmly connected as to seem not prosthesis but natural shiny appendage. Think of the colorful Dr. Seuss characters with horns for mouths. The sheer force and volume of breath emitted by a horn section confirms the illusion (if it is only that) that instrument and body are one, as do the sputtering lips and all the saliva, which the performers unabashedly expectorate through indiscreet valves in their brassy chins.

During a work by Eric Ewazen, a crane fly (in the South, "skeeter-eater") hovered at the proscenium. He never broke the invisible barrier that separated him from the performers, as if the air was too full of sound for his spindly body to penetrate it. As children, we would throw straw against the stiff autumn wind and see how far it would blow back, how it would spiral along the way. But unlike that aerobatic straw, the fly held steady, even when the horns began a heavily syncopated, hard-breathing rhythm. Did his maple seed wings register a change in the weather? Was it a strain for him to ride into the wind?

And what about the mosquito, one of several that had immigrated through the open concert hall windows and into orbit around the perspiring July bodies of the audience. It circled us fixedly as a moon. Imagine its strength as it revolved uninhibited by the atmospheric undulations, the waves on waves and angles of waves of sound continually rearranging across the vast space surrounding it. How could it not be affected by all that breathy hornplay, or is it like us, so tiny in comparison to the earth and thus utterly unaware of the planet's hurling, raging motion? Jacob, my youngest, grabbed at the mosquito and missed. There was a simoom at the level of the Hoo in Hooville, but like the crane fly facing the Ewazen headwind, the mosquito held its course.

(Why have I made the crane fly a "he" and the mosquito an "it"? Thus pronouns betray the subconscious: sympathy for the skeeter-eater, contempt for the vampire.)

Now it lights on the ear of the lady in front of us. She is unaware. "How daur ye set fit upon her--/ Sae fine a lady?" What would Bobby Burns do? Decorum trumps chivalry in the concert hall as it did during that Presbyterian sermon. I dare not swat, the band plays, the bug slurps his fill of rank, mercurial rozet.

Despite the humidity and the crowd, the evening's heavy vapor and the acres dense with sanguine bodies, there were no mosquitoes at the midsummer bluegrass festival. We came prepared with an arsenal of toxins, and none was needed. My mother, who despised that "whiny music," would have had an explanation: the noise drove them away. It's a variation on the Pied Piper tale, the fiddler's imitation hen-clucks sent the bugs fleeing to certain death in the nearby creek water. But mosquitoes surely have a taste for the high lonesome sound. Their alarming drone, pitched at the upper register of human hearing, is echoed in bluegrass music's falsetto tenor. Summer evening porches and pastures being the primary stages for bluegrass, mosquitoes must be aficionados of the form, as are crickets and katydids. So why hadn't they descended on Walsh's farm to dance and feed?

Scores of swallows banked and swooped along the belly of mist lowering just above the crowd. Jacob declared that the mosquitoes were no match for them. The birds' display was convincing, a flying circus to rival the Star Wars space combat that thrilled me in my childhood, or more recently the plucky pilots from the remnants of Galactica's fleet diving into dogfights among computer-generated swarms of sleek Cylon ships. No militant music here, however, no John Williams jubilation. These swallows were the visual of a mandolin's pyrotechnics. Mosquitoes perished to the tune of "Roanoke."

I'm tempted to follow the swallows now, because the music of a Swinburne poem momentarily overcomes the fiddles and mandolins, the way one AM signal gives way in the night to another. It's "Itylus" I'm hearing, in which the nightingale pleas with her sister, the swallow, not to forget their tragic story. Plaintive music is the lyric's principal offering:

O sister, sister, thy first-begotten!
The hands that cling and the feet that follow,
The voice of the child's blood crying yet,
Who hath remembered me? Who hath forgotten?
Thou hast forgotten, O summer swallow,
But the world shall end when I forget.

My topic is insect music, not birdsong, but I am a sucker for well-wrought sentimentality. That is the harmonic convergence of bluegrass music and Victorian poetics. The Victorians, like the Bluegrass Boys, could let down their guard, list and even founder on a shoal of tears, and somehow remain brilliant technicians and perceptive humanists.

Among the mosquitoes, a single survivor descends from the cloud of music, ozone, and poetry. It lights on the back of my hand, on the long blue vein that snakes up from my wrist and curves below my index finger knuckle. What is there to dread, I ask, besides the inconvenience of an itch? West Nile virus was a tempest in a teapot. Here we have no malaria. This survivor is decked in black and white, tuxedoed, true to the dandified nature of the vampire. I will call him Polidori, after the father of English vampires. And who wouldn't sympathize with a poor Polidori, always in the shadow of another: doctor to Lord

Byron, forgotten handmaiden to *Frankenstein*, suicide uncle of the Rossettis (D.G., Christina, and William Michael)? He drinks up. Meanwhile the fiddler says he'll take requests. Above, the swallows are in perpetual motion.

To listen to music is to be in a state of grace. It's temporary, though with my earbuds screwed deep into my skull, I jog along and fully succumb to the illusion that Beethoven's Ninth swells from within and completely encompasses me. What force interposes itself with a noise grating enough, a bite powerful enough, a sight spectacular enough, to disrupt the illusion? "Freude, schöner Gotterfunken,,,"

"…and then it was/ There interposed a Fly," angling at sweatbeads on my nose. From the human perspective the insect is an interrupter, at best a distraction, at worst the harbinger of destruction. Not even the deathbed aura is impregnable, as Dickinson's poem demonstrates, where it's the bluebottle's brash bumbling that shutters the light. No fly in literature bears a greater burden, all the more so because like the microscopic fauna that will initiate the demise of most of us, it does so unwittingly, an "uncertain" interloper, a naïve catalyst. Call to mind photos of famine. Always the dusty child, the distended belly, the fly crawling on his lip or eyebrow. As a boy, I wondered why every American couldn't adopt a famine victim. My family was working class, wealthy by comparison to the people we saw in ads from CARE and UNICEF. Our flies stayed in the barn and on the cows' backs. When they ventured to the porch, we had swatters and swags of poisonous yellow paper to suspend from the rails: alluring, silent Siren songs. That a child could be so desperately hungry and hot that a fly's prickly, filthy feet didn't cause him to twitch called for dramatic acts of charity. The evangelical Fanny Crosby hymn commanded us to "rescue the perishing, care for the dying." Bring all the needy into the homes of people whose needs were orders of magnitude smaller, where "pestilence" has downgraded to "pest."

I wave away the nuisance, my stride does not break, and I turn up the volume to mend the breach the fly made in my joyous wall of sound. But I'm barely listening because I'm thinking of the Israelites in Egypt. "And there came a grievous swarm of flies into the house of Pharaoh, and into his servants' houses, and into all the land of Egypt: the land was corrupted by reason of the swarm of flies." Mere pests, even in multitudes, couldn't soften a tyrant's heart. It would take nine plagues altogether, the flies were only number four, and one wonders whether the God of Israel should have chosen a different strategy. Should have caused, for example, the Pharaoh to feel compassion for an Israelite? And behold, the Lord God made the heavens to open and a host of swallows poured forth like rain, singing, "Was den grossen Ring bewohnet/ Huldige der Sympathie!" They fed upon the lice, the flies, the locusts, and with the balm of their wings soothed the boils of the Egyptians, the lash-marks of the sons and daughters of Abraham. Lo, spake the Pharaoh, my heart is heavy within me, for I have caused pain and more pain. My comfort has been purchased with the blood of these my sisters and brothers. The world shall end when I forget the sorrows I have wrought.

Then again a fly is usually just a fly, pesky, not a pestilence. Most escape from wanton boys and girls who would kill them for sport. They evade our clumsy swats and return for more of the epidermal giblets they were after in the first place. So it is with the fly that accompanies Beethoven and me on this run. I cannot hear its insistent droning, but neither can I ignore its role in today's performance of the symphony, the one I attend as I run. It's one of hundreds of recorded Ninths re-played during this twenty-four hours around the globe. Someone listens as he chops bok choy and waves away flies, someone as she calculates mortgage interest and flicks the pest off her soda straw. Someone as he studies the score for the concert he'll conduct next fall. He feels a twinge in his side, the first detectable salvo from the tiny animalcules that will carry him off the following summer. There will be a vigil in a sterile hospital room. It is night. The heart monitor keeps rhythm. In counterpoint, a bluebottle seeking light thumps, thumps, thumps against the double-paned window.

"Play this one allegro giocoso and forte throughout, for he is a fröhlicher Landmann, a happy farmer. That's why he hums in G major. That's why you lift your bow so often, why there are staccato notes, light and strong, why you start each phrase with an up-bow. In Suzuki we call it the up-bow song."

On a half-size violin Jacob follows his teacher. "Remember the up-bow. Yes, it's hard. This will be work. Remember the up-bow. But keep it light, giocoso, be jocular. The farmer is happy that the winter is over. His horses are merry, his cows and sheep are merry, his bees (remember the up-bow) go in search of flowers."

Outside a bee hovers near a hole in the decaying shingles of our house. A small knot of energy, it pops inside, and is followed by another, and another, and another, a row of eighth notes dancing down the tunnel. In equal numbers they exit the same opening. Carpenter bees. I press my ear to the wall. They resonate with the Happy Farmer. Work without ceasing, whistle or in this case hum while you do so. These bees are dwarves, miners rather than carpenters. They build by destruction, sectioning off shafts and rooms with the tiny timbers they've milled in their mandibles, cute percussion, a sandblock rhythm-making as in Kindergarten orchestras.

I watch them and listen until the end of the violin lesson. Then I plug the hole with Duck tape. A carpenter bee won't find another way out. Huis clos. No pesticide is needed, no swatter, although smashing a mosquito or fly in plain view seems more honest than quickly, antiseptically entombing a colony of bees.

Put your ear to the wall. That's just the pulse of blood through the arteries of your head.

Giocoso. Up-bow. After all, these were not the farmer's honeybees, not the ones you would watch from your perch in the mimosa, that tree from the pages of Dr. Seuss, with its wavy limbs and silk pom-pom blossoms. You would lie along a limb and put your eye so close to a flower you could see the bee's tongue uncurl. The bee would touch down gently, like a mosquito on an old lady's ear, and nuzzle into the pink. Now you turn your ear to the flower. Upbow. Dozens of bees swarm the mimosa, Albizia julibrissin, gul-i-abrisham, "silk flower." I have little Latin, zero Persian, but those are the sounds of a mimosa filled with honeybees.

Play this one allegro giocoso and forte to the finish.

Fomite
Burlington, Vermont

Fomite is a literary press whose authors and artists explore the human condition -- political, cultural, personal and historical -- in poetry and prose.

A fomite is a medium capable of transmitting infectious organisms from one individual to another.

"The activity of art is based on the capacity of people to be infected by the feelings of others." Tolstoy, *What is Art?*

AlphaBetaBestiario - Antonello Borra
Animals have always understood that mankind is not fully at home in the world. Bestiaries, hoping to teach, send out warnings. This one, of course, aims at doing the same.

Flight and Other Stories - Jay Boyer
In *Flight and Other Stories,* we're with the fattest woman on earth as she draws her last breaths and her soul ascends toward its final reward. We meet a divorcee who can fly for no more effort than flapping her arms. We follow a middle-aged butler whose love affair with a young woman leads him first to the mysteries of bondage, and then to the pleasures of malice. Story by story, we set foot into worlds so strange as to seem all but surreal, yet everything feels familiar, each moment rings true. And that's when we recognize we're in the hands of one of America's truly original talents.

Improvisational Arguments - Anna Faktorovich
Improvisational Arguments is written in free verse to capture the essence of modern problems and triumphs. The poems clearly relate short, frequently humorous and occasionally tragic, stories about travels to exotic and unusual places, fantastic realms, abnormal jobs, artistic innovations, political objections, and misadventures with love.

Fomite
Burlington, Vermont

Loisaida - Dan Chodorokoff

Catherine, a young anarchist estranged from her parents and squatting in an abandoned building on New York's Lower East Side is fighting with her boyfriend and conflicted about her work on an underground newspaper. After learning of a developer's plans to demolish a community garden, Catherine builds an alliance with a group of Puerto Rican community activists. Together they confront the confluence of politics, money, and real estate that rule Manhattan. All the while she learns important lessons from her great-grandmother's life in the Yiddish anarchist movement that flourished on the Lower East Side at the turn of the century. In this coming of age story, family saga, and tale of urban politics, Dan Chodorkoff explores the "principle of hope", and examines how memory and imagination inform social change.

Still Time - Michael Cocchiarale

Still Time is a collection of twenty-five short and shorter stories exploring tensions that arise in a variety of contemporary relationships: a young boy must deal with the wrath of his out-of-work father; a woman runs into a man twenty years after an awkward sexual encounter; a wife, unable to conceive, imagines her own murder, as well as the reaction of her emotionally distant husband; a soon-to-be tenured English professor tries to come to terms with her husband's shocking return to the religion of his youth; an assembly line worker, married for thirty years, discovers the surprising secret life of his recently hospitalized wife. Whether a few hundred or a few thousand words, these and other stories in the collection depict characters at moments of deep crisis. Some feel powerless, overwhelmed—unable to do much to change the course of their lives. Others rise to the occasion and, for better or for worse, say or do the thing that might transform them for good. Even in stories with the most troubling of endings, there remains the possibility of redemption. For each of the characters, there is still time.

Loosestrife - Greg Delanty

This book is a chronicle of complicity in our modern lives, a witnessing of war and the destruction of our planet. It is also an attempt to adjust the more destructive blueprint myths of our society. Often our cultural memory tells us to keep quiet about the aspects that are most challenging to our ethics, to forget the violations we feel and tremors that keep us distant and numb.

Fomite
Burlington, Vermont

Carts and Other Stories - Zdravka Evtimova

Roots and wings are the key words that best describe the short story collection, *Carts and Other Stories,* by Zdravka Evtimova. The book is emotionally multilayered and memorable because of its internal power, vitality and ability to touch both the heart and your mind. Within its pages, the reader discovers new perspectives true wealth, and learns to see the world with different eyes. The collection lives on the borders of different cultures. *Carts and Other Stories* will take the reader to wild and powerful Bulgarian mountains, to silver rains in Brussels, to German quiet winter streets and to wind bitten crags in Afghanistan. This book lives for those seeking to discover the beauty of the world around them, and will have them appreciating what they have — and perhaps what they have lost as well.

The Listener Aspires to the Condition of Music - Barry Goldensohn

"I know of no other selected poems that selects on one theme, but this one does, charting Goldensohn's career-long attraction to music's performance, consolations and its august, thrilling, scary and clownish charms. Does all art aspire to the condition of music as Pater claimed, exhaling in a swoon toward that one class act? Goldensohn is more aware than the late 19th century of the overtones of such breathing: his poems thoroughly round out those overtones in a poet's lifetime of listening."

John Peck, poet, editor, Fellow of the American Academy of Rome

The Co-Conspirator's Tale - Ron Jacobs

There's a place where love and mistrust are never at peace; where duplicity and deceit are the universal currency. *The Co-Conspirator's Tale* takes place within this nebulous firmament. There are crimes committed by the police in the name of the law. Excess in the name of revolution. The combination leaves death in its wake and the survivors struggling to find justice in a San Francisco Bay Area noir by the author of the underground classic *The Way the Wind Blew:A History of the Weather Underground* and the novel *Short Order Frame Up.*

Fomite
Burlington, Vermont

When You Remember Deir Yassin - R.L Green

When You Remember Deir Yassin is a collection of poems by R. L. Green, an American Jewish writer, on the subject of the occupation and destruction of Palestine. Green comments: "Outspoken Jewish critics of Israeli crimes against humanity have, strangely, been called 'anti-Semitic' as well as the hilariously illogical epithet 'self-hating Jews.' As a Jewish critic of the Israeli government, I have come to accept these accusations as a stamp of approval and a badge of honor, signifying my own fealty to a central element of Jewish identity and ethics: one must be a lover of truth and a friend to the oppressed, and stand with the victims of tyranny, not with the tyrants, despite tribal loyalty or self-advancement. These poems were written as expressions of outrage, and of grief, and to encourage my sisters and brothers of every cultural or national grouping to speak out against injustice, to try to save Palestine, and in so doing, to reclaim for myself my own place as part of the Jewish people." Poems in the original English are accompanied by Arabic and Hebrew translations.

Roadworthy Creature, Roadworthy Craft - Kate Magill

Words fail but the voice struggles on. The culmination of a decade's worth of performance poetry, *Roadworthy Creature, Roadworthy Craft* is Kate Magill's first full-length publication. In lines that are sinewy yet delicate, Magill's poems explore the terrain where idea and action meet, where bodies and words commingle to form a strange new flesh, a breathing text, an "I" that spirals outward from itself.

Zinsky the Obscure - Ilan Mochari

"If your childhood is brutal, your adulthood becomes a daily attempt to recover: a quest for ecstasy and stability in recompense for their early absence." So states the 30-year-old Ariel Zinsky, whose bachelor-like lifestyle belies the torturous youth he is still coming to grips with. As a boy, he struggles with the beatings themselves; as a grownup, he struggles with the world's indifference to them. *Zinsky the Obscure* is his life story, a humorous chronicle of his search for a redemptive ecstasy through sex, an entrepreneurial sports obsession, and finally, the cathartic exercise of writing it all down. Fervently recounting both the comic delights and the frightening horrors of a life in which he feels – always – that he is not like all the rest, Zinsky survives the worst and relishes the best with idiosyncratic style, as his heartbreak turns into self-awareness and his suicidal ideation into self-regard. A vivid evocation of the all-consuming nature of lust and ambition – and the forces that drive them.

Fomite
Burlington, Vermont

Visiting Hours - Jennifer Anne Moses

Visiting Hours, a novel-in-stories, explores the lives of people not normally met on the page---AIDS patients and those who care for them. Set in Baton Rouge, Louisiana, and written with large and frequent dollops of humor, the book is a profound meditation on faith and love in the face of illness and poverty.

Love's Labours - Jack Pulaski

In the four stories and two novellas that comprise *Love's Labors* the protagonists Ben and Laura, discover in their fervid romance and long marriage their interlocking fates, and the histories that preceded their births. They also learned something of the paradox between love and all the things it brings to its beneficiaries: bliss, disaster, duty, tragedy, comedy, the grotesque, and tenderness.

Ben and Laura's story is also the particularly American tale of immigration to a new world. Laura's story begins in Puerto Rico, and Ben's lineage is Russian-Jewish. They meet in City College of New York, a place at least analogous to a melting pot. Laura struggles to rescue her brother from gang life and heroin. She is mother to her younger sister; their mother Consuelo is the financial mainstay of the family and consumed by work. Despite filial obligations, Laura aspires to be a serious painter. Ben writes, cares for and is caught up in the misadventures and surreal stories of his younger schizophrenic brother. Laura is also a story teller as powerful and enchanting as Scheherazade. Ben struggles to survive such riches, and he and Laura endure.

The Derivation of Cowboys & Indians
- Joseph D. Reich

The Derivation of Cowboys & Indians represents a profound journey, a breakdown of The American Dream from a social, cultural, historical, and spiritual point of view. Reich examines in concise!detail the loss of the collective unconscious, commenting on our!contemporary postmodern culture with its self-interested excesses, on where and how things all go wrong, and how social/political practice rarely meets its original proclamations and promises. Reich's surreal and self-effacing satire brings this troubling message home. *The Derivations of Cowboys & Indians* is a desperate search and struggle for America's literal, symbolic, and spiritual home.

Fomite
Burlington, Vermont

Kasper Planet: Comix and Tragix - Peter Schumann

The British call him Punch, the Italians, Pulchinello, the Russians, Petruchka, the Native Americans, Coyote. These are the figures we may know. But every culture that worships authority will breed a Punch-like, anti-authoritan resister. Yin and yang -- it has to happen. The Germans call him Kasper. Truth-telling and serious pranking are dangerous professions when going up against power. Bradley Manning sits naked in solitary; Julian Assange is pursued by Interpol, Obama's Department of Justice, and Amazon.com. But -- in contrast to merely human faces -- masks and theater can often slip through the bars. Consider our American Kaspers: Charlie Chaplin, Woody Guthrie, Abby Hoffman, the Yes Men -- theater people all, utilizing various forms to seed critique. Their profiles and tactics have evolved along with those of their enemies. Who are the bad guys that call forth the Kaspers? Over the last half century, with his Bread & Puppet Theater, Peter Schumann has been tireless in naming them, excoriating them with Kasperdom....from Marc Estrin's Foreword to Planet Kasper

Travers' Inferno - L.E. Smith

In the 1970's churches began to burn in Burlington, Vermont. Travers' Inferno places these fires in the dizzying zeitgeist of aggressive utopian movements, distrust in authority, escapist alternative life styles, and a parasite news media. Its characters – colorful, damaged, comical, and tragic – are seeking meaning through desperate acts. Protagonist Travers Jones is grounded in the transcendent, mystified by the opposite sex, haunted by an absent father, and directed by an uncle with a grudge. Around him: secessionist Québecois murdering, pilfering and burning; changing alliances; violent deaths; confused love making; and a belligerent cat.

Views Cost Extra - L.E. Smith

Views that inspire, that calm, or that terrify – all come at some cost to the viewer. In Views Cost Extra you will find a New Jersey high school preppy who wants to inhabit the "perfect" cowboy movie, a rural mailman disgusted with the residents of his town who wants to live with the penguins, an ailing screen writer who strikes a deal with Johnny Cash to reverse an old man's failures, an old man who ponders a young man's suicide attempt, a one-armed blind blues singer who wants to reunite with the car that took her arm on the assembly line -- and more. These stories suggest that we must pay something to live even ordinary lives.

Fomite
Burlington, Vermont

My God, What Have We Done? - Susan Weiss

In a world afflicted with war, toxicity, and hunger, does what we do in our private lives really matter? Fifty years after the creation of the atomic bomb at Los Alamos, newlyweds Pauline and Clifford visit that once-secret city on their honeymoon, compelled by Pauline's fascination with Oppenheimer, the soulful scientist. The two stories emerging from this visit reverberate back and forth between the loneliness of a new mother at home in Boston and the isolation of an entire community dedicated to the development of the bomb. While Pauline struggles with unforeseen challenges of family life, Oppenheimer and his crew reckon with forces beyond all imagining.

Finally the years of frantic research on the bomb culminate in a stunning test explosion that echoes a rupture in the couple's marriage. Against the backdrop of a civilization that's out of control, Pauline begins to understand the complex, potentially explosive physics of personal relationships.

At once funny and dead serious, *My God, What Have We Done?* sifts through the ruins left by the bomb in search of a more worthy human achievement.

As It Is On Earth - Peter M. Wheelwright

Four centuries after the Reformation Pilgrims sailed up the down-flowing watersheds of New England, Taylor Thatcher, irreverent scion of a fallen family of Maine Puritans, is still caught in the turbulence.

In his errant attempts to escape from history, the young college professor is further unsettled by his growing attraction to Israeli student Miryam Bluehm as he is swept by Time through the "family thing" – from the tangled genetic and religious history of his New England parents to the redemptive birthday secret of Esther Fleur Noire Bishop, the Cajun-Passamaquoddy woman who raised him and his younger half-cousin/half-brother, Bingham.

The landscapes, rivers, and tidal estuaries of Old New England and the Mayan Yucatan are also casualties of history in Thatcher's story of Deep Time and re-discovery of family on Columbus Day at a high-stakes gambling casino, rising in resurrection over the starlit bones of a once-vanquished Pequot Indian Tribe.

Fomite
Burlington, Vermont

The Empty Notebook Interrogates Itself

- Susan Thomas

The Empty Notebook began its life as a very literal metaphor for a few weeks of what the poet thought was
writer's block, but was really the struggle of an eccentric
persona to take over her working life. It won. And for the
next three years everything she wrote came to her in the
voice of the Empty Notebook, who, as the notebook
began to fill itself, became rather opinionated, changed
gender, alternately acted as bully and victim, had many bizarre adventures in exotic locales and developed a somewhat politically-incorrect
attitude. It then began to steal the voices and forms of other poets and
tried to immortalize itself in various poetry reviews. It is now thrilled to
collect itself in one slim volume.

Made in the USA
Charleston, SC
02 November 2012